A STAR VISITOR

"Katarina Witt is here at camp, in the locker room? She's really here?" Jill repeated, completely blown away by the news.

"Don't be silly," Danielle retorted. "Katarina Witt's not here."

"Yes, she is," Haley insisted. "Hey, Jill, aren't you going to try to meet her?"

Jill hesitated.

"Go on, or you'll miss your chance," Haley urged her. "Once everyone else knows she's here, she'll be mobbed."

"Okay, I'll go," Jill said. "The locker room?"

"The locker room!" Haley repeated.

"I want to get Katarina's autograph too," Danielle said suddenly.

"Sure," Haley agreed. "But let Jill be the first one to meet her. It's only fair, since she is Jill's favorite skater."

Jill couldn't believe it. She was actually going to meet her idol, face-to-face. The 1984 and 1988 Olympic gold-medal winner. Wait till she told Kevin and Bronya about this. She turned around and ran in her stocking feet to the locker room . . .

SKATING CAMP

Melissa Lowell

Created by Parachute Press

A SKYLARK BOOK
NEW YORK · TORONTO · LONDON · SYDNEY · AUCKLAND

RL 5.0, 009-012

SKATING CAMP
A Skylark Book / July 1994

Skylark Books is a registered trademark of Bantam Books, a division
of Bantam Doubleday Dell Publishing Group, Inc. Registered in U.S.
Patent and Trademark Office and elsewhere.

Series design: Barbara Berger

ISBN 0-553-48198-3

Published simultaneously in the United States and Canada

Bantam Books are published by Bantam Books, a division of Bantam Doubleday
Dell Publishing Group, Inc. Its trademark, consisting of the words "Bantam Books"
and the portrayal of a rooster, is Registered in U.S. Patent and Trademark Office
and in other countries. Marca Registrada. Bantam Books, 1540 Broadway, New
York, New York 10036.

PRINTED IN THE UNITED STATES OF AMERICA

OPM 0 9 8 7 6 5 4 3 2

1

Dear Jill,

I can't believe it! In just five days, six hours, and twenty minutes, I, Nikki Simon, will get to see you again at Redwood Skating Camp. It'll sure be the longest five days of my life. . . . I bet you feel the same way.

Speaking of bets—Dani, Tori, and I bet a Super Sundae's ice-cream special (even though Dani's on a diet) on your summer plans. Dani said you'd stay in Denver at the Ice Academy so that you could continue your serious training for the Olympics. Tori was sure you'd head to SummerSkate in Michigan because Kristi Yamaguchi and Paul Wylie are there, coaching that seminar on surviv-

*ing international competition. But I knew you'd
do anything to be with us! Tori and Dani chipped
in to buy me a big banana split—it was great!*

*I'm so excited you're coming to camp. But you
should know that Tori's mom thinks you're nuts
to turn down a chance to meet all the skating
greats. She told Tori next year she'd better qualify
for SummerSkate or else.*

OR ELSE what? Tori wonders.

*The good news about Tori's mom, though, is
that she finally said that Tori could go to camp
with us. You did a good thing, Jill, last winter
in Lake Placid, when you convinced Tori to stop
letting her mother push her around. Tori's really
learning to stick up for herself.*

*Haley Arthur (remember her?) is coming to
skating camp too. She's been hanging with us
for a while now and is lots of fun. She's a great
pairs skater too. You will really love her.*

*I wish I had time to fill you in on more of
the Silver Blades' gossip, but Mom isn't feeling
well and I have to help Dad fix dinner. So see
you in a few days.*

> *Heaps of love and hugs,*
> *Nikki*

*P.S. I can't wait to watch you skate. I'll bet you're
really awesome now, and much better than us.*

P.P.S. Now it's just five days, five hours, and ten minutes before we get to talk IN PERSON!

Jill Wong leaned back in her airplane seat and grinned as she finished rereading her friend Nikki Simon's letter. She stretched her legs to ease out a cramp. She'd had her usual tough early-morning skating session at the Ice Academy that day and had rushed from the rink to the Denver airport without cooling down. Now she was in the air, on her way to Camp Redwood in northern California. It had been months since she'd seen her best friends in Silver Blades, and she couldn't wait till they were all together again. Even though Jill was very excited about going to Camp Redwood, she'd taken a long time to decide how to spend her summer. In fact, Jill thought as she pulled her straight black hair into a ponytail, Nikki had come very close to losing the bet she'd made with Danielle Panati and Tori Carsen. Part of Jill had really wanted to go to SummerSkate. But as soon as she was set to go, she'd started thinking of her old friends from Silver Blades having fun at camp together. Jill had made lots of new friends at the Ice Academy—especially her roommate Bronya Comaneau, and Kevin Olsen— but she missed talking to Nikki and Danielle and Tori in person. The three girls were her best friends, and they always had a great time together.

Jill stared out at the puffy clouds and smiled as she

pictured the look on Tori's face when she saw Jill land a perfect double axel. Tori would be so surprised! Tori and Jill always tried to outdo each other on the ice. Sometimes their competitiveness had caused problems between them, but Jill also knew that it had made each of them a better and stronger skater.

And it would be great seeing Danielle again. Jill and Danielle had been friends since third grade, longer than any of the others. Jill missed Danielle's sensible approach to things and her loyalty. She was someone Jill could always count on.

Jill glanced at Nikki's letter a final time before tucking it into her duffel bag. Nikki had only moved to Seneca Hills last fall, but Jill felt as close to her as she did to Tori and Danielle. Maybe even closer, Jill realized. Jill had been the first in Silver Blades to become friends with Nikki, and it was Nikki who'd been the most understanding when Jill had had problems being the "new kid" at a new ice rink. Of Jill's three friends, Nikki was the one who had written Jill the most letters at school.

The airplane cabin was cold, and Jill pulled her worn red sweatshirt out of her bag and draped it around her shoulders. She loved this sweatshirt. It had been a going-away gift from all the skaters in Silver Blades when she'd left five months ago. It was oversized, with the words *Silver Blades* on the front, and *Seneca Hills, Pennsylvania* on the back. Even though her old skating club's colors were light blue and white, the sweatshirt was red. Until recently she used to wear red every single day.

As the plane approached the airport, Jill fastened her seat belt. Her heart began to beat quicker. She was so excited, she could hardly stay in her seat. I can't wait, Jill thought. It'll be just like it used to be—tons of fun with the best friends I've ever had!

"Hey, Jill! We're over here!"

"Nikki!" Jill shouted, immediately spotting her friend in the crowded camp parking lot.

Tori, Danielle, and Nikki rushed over to the bus. Their arms closed around Jill in an enormous hug. She was almost swept off her feet.

"I thought you'd never get here," Danielle cried.

"Dani, you look great!" Jill said. "You've lost weight."

Danielle blushed. "Thanks. Dieting has been a real pain, but I guess it's working."

"Jill, we've been here for ages waiting for you," Tori interrupted. Her clear blue eyes were gleaming with excitement, and for once her curly blond hair looked messed up. "We haven't even found our bunk yet!"

Nikki threw open her arms to give Jill another warm hug. "I'm so psyched you're here, Jill!"

"Me too. It's so awesome to see all you guys!" Jill exclaimed. "Hey, don't we have to check in or something?"

Danielle pointed to a table outside a long wooden

building. A white sign above the door said DINING HALL. A long line of campers was forming to the left of the table. "Over there," Danielle said.

As the four girls joined the line, Tori planted her perfectly manicured hands on her hips and shook her head. "I don't believe it, Jill. You're not wearing red!" Tori smoothed her own white shorts and looked approvingly at Jill.

Jill looked down at her pale-pink minidress and laughed. "I should have known it wouldn't take long for the Silver Blades' fashion queen to notice. Do you like it?"

"I love it!" Tori said. "But I can't believe you actually own clothes that aren't red."

"You don't like red anymore?" Danielle sounded disappointed. "I guess everything changes."

"Don't worry, Dani. It's still my fave. I just thought I'd try something different." Jill grinned. "Now I wear red every *other* day of the week."

"Wearing red or not, you're still the same old Jill," Nikki said warmly. Nikki was wearing sunglasses, a filmy lavender cotton skirt and matching tank top, and delicate sandals that laced up her ankles. A breeze gusted off the lake and blew Nikki's thick brown hair off her face.

"Thanks, Nikki," Jill said, smiling at her friend. "So, how's your mom?"

"My mom?" Nikki looked confused.

"You said in your letter she was sick," Jill reminded her.

Nikki shook her head and looked puzzled for a moment. "She's not sick, not really," Nikki said quickly, then grabbed Jill's arm. "Oh, look, there's Haley." Nikki quickly waved Haley over.

A moment later Jill found herself looking into a pair of enormous brown eyes. Although she and Haley had never been friends when Jill belonged to Silver Blades, Haley's red hair, single earring, and boyish style were certainly unforgettable, and so was her skill as a pairs skater. Today Haley wore baggy black shorts and an oversized white T-shirt.

"Hi." Jill smiled at the other girl. "I've been hearing a lot about you in everyone's letters."

Haley laughed, showing a friendly smile.

The line inched forward. Haley helped Tori roll one of her three large matching suitcases across the ground.

"Where's Alex?" Jill asked Nikki. "I can't wait to see you two skate together." She shielded her brown eyes from the sun and peered around the crowd, looking for Nikki's cute skating partner. "All I see are girls. What happened to the guys? Isn't this a coed camp?"

Nikki laughed. "Alex is over with the guys, on the other side of the parking lot." She pointed toward the tennis courts.

"He's with Patrick," Haley chimed in. "Patrick McGuire, my new pairs partner. He's easy to spot. We look exactly alike."

True to Haley's word, Patrick *was* easy to spot. Jill immediately noticed his red hair in the crowd of guys. They were all milling around another registration table. Next to Patrick was Alex Beekman, looking tan and confident, as always. And right next to Alex, Jill noticed a tall guy with curly blond hair wearing a faded denim shirt. He had a beat-up green knapsack over his shoulder, and his brown cowboy boots looked broken in and worn.

"Who's the guy next to Alex? I haven't seen him on the skating circuit," Jill asked Nikki.

Nikki pushed up her sunglasses and shrugged. "I don't know. He's not from Silver Blades, and I don't think he's from any of the East Coast clubs."

"He's cute," Danielle remarked.

"Where are the guys' bunks?" Tori asked.

Nikki pulled a map of the camp out of the pocket of her skirt. "On the other side of the gravel road by the tennis courts," she said a minute later. "The girls' bunks are by the soccer field and the horse stables."

Jill glanced across the road and noticed some low, one-story redwood buildings. Those were probably the boys' bunks. Farther down the road Jill spotted a shimmering blue lake and a large building with a high, domed roof that sparkled in the afternoon sun. That must be where the skating rink is, Jill thought. She couldn't wait to see it.

"Does anyone know how many girls we'll have in *our* bunk?" Danielle asked.

"Eight, I think," Tori answered. "Five of us, plus three other girls."

The girls were just about at the head of the line.

Jill dug into her duffel bag and pulled out a folder with her forms, health certificate, and personal data sheet.

Haley was right in front of her. As they approached the table where the counselors were sitting, Haley produced a wad of papers from the roomy pockets in her shorts. She handed them to one of the counselors behind the table. A pink-striped gum wrapper and a couple of pieces of cellophane poked out from between the forms. The counselor made a disgusted face at Haley's mess and then picked up the papers and straightened them out with her hand.

"Haley Arthur?" the counselor said as she looked at the paperwork.

"In person," Haley replied, rocking back and forth on the heels of her combat boots.

The counselor flipped her dark brown braid over her shoulder as she continued reading the forms. The name tag on her camp T-shirt said MEREDITH "MERRY" WALKER.

Merry looked up.

"Haley, you seem to have a very strange collection of hobbies."

Jill glanced at Haley, who was trying to keep a straight face.

"What's she talking about?" Danielle demanded. "Haley, what did you put down on that information sheet?"

"Only the truth," Haley replied innocently.

"Well, if that's the case," Merry said with a grin, "maybe you'd be better off at another camp. For one thing I don't think we keep any boa constrictors handy for our campers to wrestle, and I sure hope you didn't bring your collection of dinosaur bones and shrunken heads to camp with you."

"Boa constrictors? Shrunken heads?" Jill repeated.

"Haley's up to something again!" Nikki confided to Jill in a giggly whisper.

"What do you mean?" Jill whispered back.

"Shhh. I'll tell you later," Nikki said. "But whatever she's going to do, I bet you it'll be funny!"

Jill nodded, feeling a little confused. Each one of her friends had her eyes fixed on Haley. Was the other girl about to do something outrageous?

"It's okay if the camp doesn't have its own snakes," Haley told Merry, her voice serious. "I brought my own boa constrictor!" She put her black backpack on the table, unzipped the top of it, and a huge snake sprang out!

Jill screamed. But Merry didn't budge. She shook her head and chuckled. "Sorry, Haley. I've been a

summer-camp counselor too long to fall for that one."
She retrieved the rubber snake and coiled it up carefully before handing it to Haley. "And since you're
in Bunk Nine, I think this is going to be a very
interesting month for me—and for you."

"Why?" Haley asked.

Merry smiled triumphantly. "Because I'm your bunk
counselor!"

2

"Come on . . . hurry up!" Jill dropped her duffel onto the porch of Bunk Nine and peered through the screen door. Then, without waiting for the others, she pulled the door open.

It took her eyes a minute to adjust to the dark interior. Along each long wall Jill saw two sets of bunk beds. And at the far end of the bunk was a single bed with a sign that said COUNSELOR'S TURF—KEEP OUT. Merry's name was scribbled in black marker under the sign.

Only the counselor's bed was made up. Every other bed had a stack of clean white sheets and pillowcases piled on top of the mattress. Multicolored braided rugs covered most of the wooden floor. A wooden table and three chairs stood in the corner.

Then Jill noticed three girls huddled together on one

of the lower bunks. In front of them, as they stared up at Jill, were their camp information packets.

Jill blinked in surprise as she recognized one of their bunkmates. But before she could say anything, the others walked in. "Carla Benson?" Nikki exclaimed.

"Tell me this is a dream," Tori whispered softly. "Pinch me."

"Well, hello there. We were wondering where you were," Carla Benson said as she got up from the bed. Her long straight blond hair hung almost to her waist. She was dressed completely in white and beige: white shirt, beige shorts, a beige headband, and white socks. Her eyes were green and her skin was as pale as Haley's.

Carla was the top-ranked skater in Blade Runners, which was Vermont's best skating club and Silver Blades' main rival. She had taken a silver medal at the Regional competition last spring where Jill had taken the gold, and Tori, the bronze. The rivalry between Tori and Carla had been very intense. Now Jill had a sinking feeling that this would be a long four weeks at camp.

Carla's two friends stood up to join her. Jill recognized them right away—Sharon Groves and Sandy Bower. They also skated with the Blade Runners. Sandy's dark curly hair was cut short, and shaggy bangs fluttered over the glasses she wore whenever she wasn't skating. Sharon had black hair and dark eyes.

"Uh—hi, Carla," Jill said quickly. "I didn't know you guys would be here."

"Don't you think the Blade Runners are good enough for Redwood Skating Camp?" Carla asked, a sly smile on her face. Jill wasn't sure if Carla was joking or not.

"And, Jill, I'm surprised you're here instead of at SummerSkate," Carla went on. "You're a rising star at the Ice Academy, after all."

Jill forced herself to meet Carla's glance. Trouble with a capital *T*, she thought. Jill made herself count to ten. When she'd first arrived at the Ice Academy, she'd had problems with two girls who were now her friends. That experience had been difficult, but it had taught her there was usually a way to work through all the fierce competition surrounding skating.

"Thanks for the compliment, Carla," Jill said, trying to sound as mature as possible. "Actually I'm at Redwood to skate and have fun. Since we all have to share this bunk for four weeks, why don't we try to get along? Okay?"

"Get along!" Tori repeated. She dropped her heavy skate bag with a loud thump. "Gimme a break. Carla doesn't know how to get along with anyone."

"That's not true," Carla snapped, and Jill saw how red her cheeks got. Sharon and Sandy exchanged an uncomfortable look.

"Hey, come on, let's call a truce and make the best of it," Jill said again.

"I'm not making the best of it," Tori said. "I'm asking for a different bunk assignment."

"We all can't have a different assignment," Nikki reminded her. "I thought we were going to stick together."

Carla cocked her head and studied the Silver Blades group before resting her gaze upon Jill. "Look, Tori, Jill's right. Let's make the best of it."

"Sandy and I picked this bunk," Sharon said, pointing to one of the four double-deckered bunk beds.

"So what do *we* do? Who's going to sleep where?" Nikki asked, looking around with a frown. Jill followed her friend's eyes. The problem was obvious. Carla had already claimed the bottom bed of one bunk, leaving only two more empty bunk beds. And there were five of them. One of them would have to share a bunk with Carla.

"Haley and I'll take one bunk," Tori spoke up, dragging her largest suitcase across the floor and scattering two small oval rugs as she went. Tori quickly dumped some of her clothes into a dresser drawer, closing it with a bang.

"I'll take an upper bed," Danielle volunteered in a loud voice. "Why don't you sleep underneath me," she added to Nikki.

"Okay," Nikki agreed, and put her flowered duffel on the thin striped mattress.

Somehow, before Jill had even realized what was happening, she'd ended up the odd one out—and the one left to share with Carla. You told your friends to

make the best of Carla, she reminded herself sternly.
It's only fair that you have to share a bunk with
her.

"Well," Carla said, glancing at Jill, "I guess we're
stuck with each other."

"I guess so." Jill forced herself to sound cheerful.
Then she tossed her red sleeping bag up onto the
upper bunk.

3

July 11

Dear Renee,

Hi, it's me—Carla, checking in from Redwood.
I've only been at camp for two days and I'm
already writing a letter to my big sister. Tell Mom
she's next—I promise!

So far camp's just okay. We're really busy all
the time. Last night we had to plan our schedules.
My bunk skates every morning from 6:30 to 8:30,
and then after breakfast we have swim instruction.
I checked out the lake today—it sure is cold! Then
we usually have other activities, such as arts and
crafts, tennis, soccer, ballet, or horseback riding.
After lunch it's two more hours of skating and
then more activities. Skating camp certainly isn't

a vacation! The good thing is that we each get a lot of lesson time—private and group lessons.

You're not going to believe who I'm sharing a bunk with—the skaters from Silver Blades! And worst of all, Tori Carsen and Jill Wong are here— the girls who I had to compete against at the Regionals last winter. Tori is as snobby as ever!

Jill's okay, but I can't believe she decided to give up SummerSkate and hang with those Silver Blades girls this summer. Jill's at the Ice Academy. Some people have all the luck—you know how much I want to train there! I hate being stuck on the waiting list, not knowing whether they're going to let me in. It's just not fair. They should have picked me, not her.

I've got to find a way to get Jill to talk to the directors of the academy about getting me in for September. Sandy and Sharon say Jill would never help me. But I think I'd have a chance if I could just pull her away from those silly friends of hers.

Write soon with news from home.
                                    Love, Carla

"Let's skate a little before dinner. We have half an hour. Who's up for it?" Jill asked. It was the second day at camp, and the girls had just returned from canoeing on the lake. Jill had already changed out of her wet bathing suit and into a purple T-shirt and denim shorts. She sat on the edge of the top bunk, dangling her legs. She wished her friends would hurry up and get their act together. Carla, Sandy, and Sharon had left ten minutes earlier to explore the camp.

"We've already skated for four hours today," Tori said as she searched for a pair of socks. She had her three suitcases of clothes stuffed into two drawers. "Without Mom around I would love to have some free time just to goof off!"

"I'll go skating," Nikki said, reaching for her skate bag.

"Let's all go to the rink," Haley said. "Even if we don't skate, the coaches said we should all choose a locker by tomorrow."

Jill grabbed her skate bag and led her friends toward the bright, airy rink.

Since she'd started skating years ago, Jill had practiced on a lot of rinks. But the one at Redwood was particularly beautiful. It had a glass ceiling and a glass back wall, which let in the brilliant rays of sunlight. Through the back wall the skaters had a view of tall evergreen trees and beautiful blooming flowers. Already Jill loved skating there.

The girls wandered past some other campers into the spacious lobby of the rink. There was a small supply shop to the left, and the locker rooms were to the right. Tori, Nikki, and Haley headed straight for the locker room to claim lockers. Danielle followed Jill to the edge of the ice.

"This is the best," Jill said, putting her arm around Danielle's shoulder. "It's so cool to be back at the rink with my friends. In some ways I feel like I never left Seneca Hills."

Danielle looked surprised. "Really?" she said. "You seem different . . . I don't know . . . I guess you seem more grown-up. I mean, I can't imagine you saying that stuff to Carla, about trying to get along and all, a couple of months ago. Not after the obnoxious way she acted at Lake Placid."

Jill laughed. "Just because I've spent a few months in Denver doesn't change who I am. I don't think Carla's a bad person deep down. She's just real competitive and doesn't know when to let up."

"I'll switch beds with you, Jill," Danielle said. "You sort of got stuck with Carla."

Jill sat down on a bench and pulled off her shoes. "Thanks," she told Danielle, "but it's okay. I mean, sharing a bunk with her isn't my first choice, but that's the breaks."

Before Danielle could respond, Sandy Bower and Sharon Groves entered the ice rink from the double doors at the end of the building. Carla wasn't with them.

"Hi," Sharon said in a friendly tone of voice.

"Ummm, hi," Jill stammered back. She hadn't expected Sharon to say anything, since the Blade Runners skaters had made a big point of avoiding Jill and her friends all day.

"So what do you think of the Ice Academy?" Sandy asked Jill. She took off her glasses and polished them on the sleeve of her gray cotton shirt.

"It's okay," Jill replied cautiously, wondering where the conversation was leading.

"I'm really interested in the Ice Academy," Sandy continued. "I don't know if I can make the cut, but I'd love to try out for the coaches next time they're on the East Coast. Carla's on the Academy's waiting list for the fall."

"Really?" Jill said, surprised. "I didn't know that. That's great for her."

"Carla really hopes to get in. There are about ten skaters on the list. It's tough waiting to find out," Sandy declared. "Do you know anything about who's going to get in?"

Jill shook her head. "Sorry."

"Hey, Jill," Sharon spoke up. "We've heard that you get to skate with famous people, and travel a lot."

"Yeah," Danielle chimed in. "You must have some great stories. We're dying to hear all about the celebrities you've met!"

"I haven't met many celebrities," Jill admitted. "I really wanted to meet Katarina Witt. She was supposed to visit, but she canceled at the last minute."

"I heard she was here last summer. She was a guest coach for a week," Sharon said.

Jill eagerly told the girls about some of the people she'd met in Colorado. Maybe Sandy and Sharon just wanted to know more about the Academy, but they were acting very friendly. And talking with them seemed to help break the tension between the two groups of girls.

Suddenly Tori, Nikki, and Haley ran out of the locker room. "Hey, Jill and Dani. Guess what!" Haley said breathlessly.

"What?" Jill called.

"You'll never guess who we just saw," Haley replied.

"Who?" Jill asked curiously.

"Katarina Witt!" Haley burst out.

"You're kidding!" Jill replied.

"Isn't it amazing?" Haley exclaimed. "Go and see for yourself. She's right here in the girls' locker room."

"Katarina Witt is here, in the locker room? She's really here?" Jill repeated, completely blown away by the news. She didn't dare believe her luck.

"Don't be silly," Danielle retorted. "Katarina Witt's not here."

"Yes, she is," Haley insisted. "Didn't you hear about it?"

Danielle shook her head, but Jill said, "We heard she was here last summer."

"Well, she's here now!" Haley announced. "Tori, Nikki, and I were coming out of the girls' locker room just as Katarina and the camp director were going in. They were talking about Katarina doing a demonstration here tomorrow."

"Wow, that's great," Sandy said, and she turned to Sharon. "Where's Carla? I wonder if she knows about this."

"How come we didn't hear about this before now?" Danielle asked suspiciously.

"A surprise, I guess," Haley answered. "Hey, Jill, aren't you going to try to meet her?"

Jill hesitated. "Go on, or you'll miss your chance," Haley urged her. "Once everyone else knows she's here, she'll be mobbed. This is the perfect time!"

"But . . . I can't just . . ." Jill stammered, her face turning red. "Tori, Nikki, come with me. Please."

"We've already seen her," Haley said. "You go. Tori told me she's your favorite skater. Maybe you could get her autograph. I bet that would impress your friends who went to SummerSkate!"

"Okay, I'll go," Jill said. "The locker room?"

"The locker room!" Haley repeated.

"I want to get Katarina's autograph too," Danielle said suddenly.

"Sure," Haley agreed. "But let Jill be the first one to meet her. It's only fair, since she is Jill's favorite."

Jill couldn't believe it. She was actually going to meet her idol, face-to-face. The 1984 and 1988 Olympic gold-medal winner. Wait till she told Kevin and Bronya about this. She turned around and ran in her stocking feet to the locker room.

4

Jill pulled on the locker-room door. It swung open, and straight ahead she could see several rows of tall, upright lockers.

Jill hurried inside, her heart still beating double-time. The door slammed behind her. Jill jumped at the noise and turned around. Then, with a gasp, she noticed what was hanging on the back of the door.

It was a lifesize poster of Katarina Witt!

Jill was speechless. It was another one of Haley's practical jokes, and Jill had fallen for it.

What a dope I am! Jill thought. She was trying to think of something clever to say to Haley, when the door opened. Haley, Tori, Nikki, and Danielle poured in. They were all laughing hysterically.

Jill felt the blood rush to her face.

"Oh, Jill!" Tori almost choked on the words. "Your face is so red—you look like you're about to explode."

Jill felt so stupid. To make matters even worse, Carla had turned up, and she and Sharon and Sandy were standing behind the Silver Blades girls. They were laughing along with everyone else.

"Haley, that was great!" Carla cried. "You really had her fooled, didn't you!"

Haley grinned, her eyes shining.

Was the whole camp in on this? Jill wondered, her embarrassment turning to anger. Still she wasn't about to give Carla the satisfaction of blowing up at Haley in front of Carla and her friends.

She forced a smile. "I guess you got me, Haley," she admitted.

Danielle gave Jill a friendly punch. "Just one of Haley's welcome-to-the-club jokes."

"Welcome to the club?" Jill repeated as a wave of hurt washed over her. She'd been friends with these girls long before Haley had come along. Wasn't she *already* part of the group?

Haley spoke up quickly. "Hey, jokes are my way of breaking the ice. You're not really angry, are you?"

Jill shook her head. "No, it's okay. It was a good joke." She tried to sound cheerful. But as the friends all left the locker room and headed back toward the ice to skate, Jill still felt foolish and left out. Her friends had been laughing at her, and there was no one she could talk to about it.

Forget about it, Jill told herself. Skating camp is

only for four weeks, then it's back to Colorado. Do you really want to ruin the little time you have with everyone by picking a fight with Haley?

No, she firmly resolved. Then she hurried back to the bench, finished lacing up her skates, and pushed off on the ice.

"This is great!" Danielle exclaimed after dinner that evening as the five girls approached the lake. "Check out that bonfire. It's huge."

"I hear music playing too," Jill added. She clapped her hands in time to the music and returned the smile of some guys seated a little distance from the fire, their backs against an enormous redwood tree. She scanned the crowd, hoping to spot that blond guy she'd seen in the parking lot.

"Let's go and sit over there," Danielle said, pointing to the far side of the bonfire, where the crowd was thinner.

They wove their way through the small groups of campers, snagging a couple of bags of marshmallows from the picnic area before settling in front of the fire.

"Did Morgan go to camp this summer?" Tori asked Haley as she piled marshmallows onto a stick.

"No, she stayed in Seneca Hills. There's a big horse show this month. I think she'll probably win a ribbon," Haley replied.

"Another ribbon!" Danielle exclaimed. "I wish I could ride a horse as well as Morgan can."

"I'm sure Morgan wishes she could skate as well as Haley does," Tori said.

"I doubt it," Haley joked. "Morgan would rather be sitting on the back of a horse when she jumps into the air, not pushing off on a thin steel blade!"

"Who's Morgan?" Jill interrupted. She had no idea who they were talking about.

"Haley's little sister," Tori answered.

"She's the best horseback rider," Danielle added. "I wish you knew her. Morgan's so spunky. You'd really love her, Jill."

"Hey, you guys, remember when Morgan brought her horse home from the stables," Haley said, "and tied it up in our front yard—"

"And it ate all your mother's daffodils!" Tori finished, collapsing into giggles.

Jill leaned back on her elbows and half listened to her friends. Since she didn't know Morgan, their story wasn't very funny. Once again, she felt left out.

She glanced over to where Nikki was sitting, on the other side of Tori and Haley. Carla, Sharon, and Sandy had just squeezed into the space to the left of Nikki. Nikki's knees were bunched up in front of her, and she had her arms wrapped around them.

I wonder why Nikki is so quiet tonight, Jill thought as the reflection from the bonfire's flames flickered across her friend's face. In the firelight Jill thought

she could see tears in Nikki's eyes. She'd try to talk
to Nikki later, when there were fewer people around,
and find out what was wrong.

Jill tuned back in to her friends' conversation.
Danielle was telling them all how excited she was
about going horseback riding at camp. "I'm glad our
counselor is the riding instructor," she announced.

"Do you ride competitively like your sister?" Jill
asked Haley.

"No." Haley shook her head. "But I like riding on the
trails. Hey, let's go riding tomorrow," she suggested.
"It'll be so much fun. What do you think, Tori?"

"Cool," Tori replied.

"I'll come too," Danielle said. She glanced at Jill.
"Oh, wait. Jill doesn't ride."

Jill didn't know what to say. Horses *terrified* her.
She'd already planned to avoid the stables the whole
four weeks of camp. But she didn't want to be left
out of the fun. Before she could say anything, the
music stopped and a counselor's whistle sounded.
The campers' chatter dropped to a low buzz.

A dark-haired counselor jumped up onto one of the
picnic tables and blew her whistle again. "My name's
Annie and I coach the pairs skaters. I've met some
of you already and I'm looking forward to working
with the rest of you."

For the first time since they'd sat down, Jill noticed
Nikki perk up and look interested.

"Tonight," Annie went on, "our second night at
camp, we have the traditional 'Welcome Ceremony.'

Each camper takes a stick and throws it into the bonfire and makes a wish out loud. It's usually something you hope will come true before camp is over. I think you'll be surprised at how many of your wishes actually become reality!"

"That's so cool," Danielle said.

Jill smiled. It did sound fun, and she was looking forward to hearing more about some of the other campers.

"I'll start!" a boy announced in a twangy Western accent. As he stepped up to the bonfire, his stick in hand, Jill caught her breath. The boy was wearing a cowboy hat, but the curls poking out from beneath the brim were unmistakable. It was the tall blond boy from the parking lot.

Nikki nudged Jill.

"I like his cowboy hat!" Haley whispered.

Jill shushed them. She wanted to hear his wish. Maybe she'd learn more about him.

"My name is Ross Barrett, and my wish is that I figure out exactly what I'm doing here and why!" He said his wish with a smile, but there was something sad about his voice. A few campers cheered and laughed.

"People shouldn't laugh," Nikki said softly. "I think he was serious."

Jill looked at Nikki, and nodded. Her friend could be so sensitive sometimes.

"Do you still like him, Jill?" Tori asked. "He looks pretty country!"

"Yeah, Jill," Danielle agreed. "Has your taste in guys changed too?"

Jill laughed. "I just think he's cute, that's all."

"I agree with Jill," Haley added. "Country guys *are* cute!"

One by one the campers stood and threw their sticks into the fire. A tiny girl with curly black hair tossed her twig into the flames and declared, "I wish I could land my axel jump this summer," and a stocky blond-haired boy announced, "I wish I could skate all day and never have to swim in the cold lake!"

As her turn drew near, Jill was worried about what she would say. If she were allowed to make a silent wish, she knew what it would be: I wish my friends and I could be as close as we were when I lived in Seneca Hills. But there was no way she could say that here, in front of her friends and all these people.

Danielle threw her stick onto the fire and declared, "I wish I could totally get over my stage fright so I could be the star of the Ice Capades someday." She sat down quickly, blushing furiously.

"Don't hold your breath," Carla muttered, just loud enough for Danielle to hear.

"I wish some people would keep their mouth shut," Tori declared softly.

Jill turned to Carla. "Okay, it's your turn," she challenged her.

Carla jumped up, tilted her chin into the air, and tossed her stick into the flames. "I wish I could win the gold in the next Regionals and be chosen to go to the Ice Academy." Carla looked right at Jill as she said that.

Haley wished she'd grow two more inches over the summer so that she'd be a better match for her new pairs partner. Patrick, who was sitting across the fire with the other guys, winked broadly at her.

Tori also wished for a gold medal at the next competition. Then she turned to Jill. "Your turn," she said.

Jill picked up a stick and twirled it around in her fingers for a moment before blurting out, "I wish I could become a really great skater. Someone who'd inspire other kids someday the way . . ." She paused and grinned down at Haley. "The way Katarina Witt inspired me!"

"All right!" Haley cheered.

Nikki stood up next. She stared into the flickering flames for a minute. "I wish that . . . ummm," she paused, and then threw her stick into the fire. Her voice was so soft that Jill had to strain to hear her. "I wish that nothing would ever change. That my parents will treat me the same way they did before my mom found out she was going to have a baby."

"A baby!" Jill's jaw dropped. Why didn't anyone tell me? She pushed her bangs out of her eyes and looked toward Tori and Danielle and Haley.

But they looked as shocked as she did. Nikki had this fantastic news and she hadn't told *any* of her friends? Why? Jill wondered. What was going on with Nikki?

5

"Your mother's pregnant?" Jill repeated for the umpteenth time since leaving the campfire. She looked at Nikki from the top of her bunk. "How long have you known? Why didn't you tell us?"

"I've only known for two months. My mom asked me to wait to tell my friends. But if I didn't say something soon, I'd burst," Nikki answered. "Remember how I used to complain a couple of months ago that my parents were acting weird? Well, it's all because my mom is going to have a baby."

"You don't sound too happy," Haley declared, squirming into her black-and-white-striped sleep shirt.

Tori stood at the door of the bathroom holding her pink toothbrush. "Yeah, why aren't you thrilled? I wish I had a brother or sister."

"I don't want to talk about it," Nikki grumbled.

She climbed into her bed and turned her back to her friends. A second later she rolled over to face them. "Okay," she said, propping herself up on her elbow. "I do want to talk. Think about it—how would any of you feel if your mother were as ancient as mine and got pregnant!"

"Ancient?" Tori looked stunned. "My mother's older than yours and she isn't ancient."

"That's ridiculous," Jill said.

Jill had six brothers and sisters, and she loved when her mother was pregnant. It was so exciting to think about a new baby. Besides that, since she'd moved to Colorado, Jill had realized how important her family's love and support were to her and her skating. Nothing thrilled her more than a letter or phone call from one of her brothers or sisters.

"My mother was older than yours when she had the twins!" Jill told Nikki.

"You're used to having lots of kids around," Nikki said. "You'll never understand how weird this is for me."

Before Jill could reply, Merry pushed open the screen door and walked into the bunk. "Hi, crew! How's the second night at camp going?" she asked, tossing her clipboard on her bed.

"Great," everyone chimed in, except Nikki.

Haley hoisted herself up to the bunk above Tori.

"Did you like the campfire?" Merry asked, kicking off her shoes and starting to get undressed. The girls talked about everyone's wishes, careful not to mention Nikki or her mother.

Carla, Sandy, and Sharon, who had been whispering together in the bathroom since returning from the campfire, wandered out and headed for their beds. Without glancing up at Jill, Carla climbed into the lower bunk.

Jill hesitated, then called down to Carla, "Good night, Carla."

Carla mumbled something.

Merry wound up a big blue alarm clock. "Okay, everybody, it's lights out. Don't forget you all have skating sessions early in the morning." Merry flipped out the lights.

Jill snuggled down in her bunk. A moment later she heard Merry cry out. Then the lights flashed on. Jill sat up straight and squinted in the glare.

"What's wrong?" Jill cried. Everyone, except Haley, was sitting upright in her bed.

"*Someone*," Merry said, staring right up at Haley, "short-sheeted my bed!"

Haley looked confused. "Short-sheeted your bed?"

"What's that?" Tori asked.

"Oh, it's a trick where you fold the top sheet in half so the person can't get their feet in under the covers," Haley said with a yawn. "But who did it?"

"Haley Arthur!" Jill couldn't quite believe her ears. "Come off it!"

"Who else but you, Haley," Danielle said, laughing.

"Right," Merry added. "And you'll get up right now and remake my bed, please. . . ."

"That's not fair. . . . I didn't . . ." Haley began. Then

she shrugged. "Though I don't blame you for thinking it is me." She climbed down from her bunk and
began to remake Merry's bed.

"Thanks," Merry said. She got up and went into the
bathroom. The minute she left the room, Carla snick-
ered. "I fooled you at your own game, Haley."

"*You* did that to Merry? And you let Haley take
the blame?" Tori exclaimed.

"Don't worry," Haley said, stripping off the sheets.
Danielle had climbed out of bed to help her. "I probably deserve this—you know, for all the jokes I've
played on other people."

"Maybe," Tori said with a sniff. "But you don't
let other people get in trouble for the stuff that you
do."

"Don't make such a big deal about it," Carla said,
yawning. "Merry isn't that upset."

Merry came out of the bathroom, and Danielle
and Haley climbed back into their bunks.

Jill couldn't believe that Haley hadn't turned Carla
in. Maybe Haley isn't as immature as I'd thought,
Jill decided.

She was still thinking about what Haley had done
when Merry turned out the light and said good night
again.

Three days after the campfire, Jill hurried toward
the rink for her afternoon group lesson. She knew

she was late—she still couldn't get the camp schedule down. She never knew if she was supposed to be wearing a bathing suit or ice skates!

Tori and Carla were already warming up when Jill arrived. The three of them had a group lesson scheduled with Robin Turner. Danielle, Sharon, and Sandy were having a group lesson on the other side of the ice with another coach named Cheryl Russell. Nikki and Haley were working with their pairs partners.

"Hurry and warm up, Jill," Robin Turner called out. "We've been waiting for you." She skated up to Jill and stopped abruptly, sending up a spray of ice particles.

"Okay," Jill said. "Sorry!" Jill had liked Robin from the start. She was an excellent coach and was also very friendly and very funny.

As Jill skated around the rink, she watched Robin working with Carla. It looked as if Carla was attempting a double Lutz. Carla launched into the difficult jump with ease, rotating two full times before landing back on the ice.

Wow, Carla's skating way better than she used to, Jill realized.

"That was great, Carla," Jill called out as Carla finished.

Carla's eyes widened at Jill's compliment. "Uh, thanks," she murmured.

"Well done," Robin agreed. She adjusted the headband that held her thick auburn hair away from her face, then turned to Jill. "Now, Jill, I want you to demonstrate your double axel for Tori. You're doing it very well, and Tori's close to being ready to try it for herself. I want her to watch yours. I'd do it myself, but I pulled a muscle last week, and the doctor has grounded me. No more leaps and spins for a while."

Jill flushed with pleasure at the praise. After all the trouble she'd had landing that particular jump at the Ice Academy, it was great to hear someone telling her how well she performed it.

She skated across the center of the rink, reviewing the jump in her mind. Then she pushed off on the edge of her skate blade, did two and a half revolutions, and landed solidly, facing backward on the correct skate.

This jump is so easy now, Jill thought. I feel as if I could do it in my sleep.

When she skated up to the coach, she could see that Robin was smiling and saying something to Tori.

"Thanks, Jill, that was great." Robin turned back to Tori. "Jill's jump was almost perfect. Watch her form and technique and try to visualize it for yourself."

Tori didn't seem very pleased. She just nodded curtly and avoided looking at Jill. Is Tori going to start acting jealous again? Jill wondered with a sinking heart. She was already having trouble with her friends; she didn't need the old rivalry with Tori.

"By the way," Robin said, "we'll be having a mini-competition in a couple of weeks, a sort of color war."

"What's that?" Carla sounded interested.

"Well, the coaches pick four team captains and give them a color—red, blue, yellow, or green. Then the captains get to choose their own teams and we have a skate-off."

"How does the skate-off work?" Jill asked.

"The coaches give each captain a list of jumps and spins the week before the competition. It's up to the captain to choose which team member will perform what move. At the skate-off each move is announced. If the yellow team member who was picked to do that move lands it better than the red team member, the yellow team gets more points. The team with the most points at the end wins color war."

"Suppose you're given a jump you can't do?" Tori asked quietly, with a quick glance in Jill's direction.

"We'll have different levels," Robin answered. "Don't worry, you won't find yourself attempting something you're not capable of. It allows you to use your technique, but it's supposed to be fun too!"

"Great," said Jill.

"Now, two of the teams, the yellow and the red, are the girls teams," Robin went on. "The boys will be blue and green—"

"Robin," Tori interrupted, "can I be one of the captains? I promise I'll do a really good job."

"Well, Tori," Robin replied, looking a little uncomfortable. "I'd already decided to make Jill and Carla the captains of the two girls teams, since they seem to be the best skaters here this summer. But I'm sure both of them would be thrilled to have you help."

"I would," Jill said eagerly.

"Oh," Tori mumbled, staring down at the ice.

Oh, boy, Jill thought. Tori really wanted to be a captain! Why had Robin singled her out for all this praise? Especially in front of Tori.

Jill wished she could say something to smooth things out. But she didn't have time to think about it. For the next two hours Robin kept them all busy practicing their spins and jumps until they were all exhausted.

Just before the end of the session Tori excused herself and skated off the ice. Jill watched her climb into the bleachers and then sit down with her chin in her hands. Jill sighed, and finished the last few moments of her lesson.

When it was over, Jill headed straight for Tori. "You okay?" she asked, reaching for a rag and wiping off the blades of her skates.

Tori glared at Jill. "No. I'm not. I'm obviously not a good enough skater these days to be a team captain."

"You're a great skater, Tori. I've just had more experience than you and more intense training. You're getting stronger all the time. . . ."

"Forget it." Tori's voice quavered. "Stop trying to make me feel better. This team-captain stuff is so unfair. Robin didn't even give me a chance. Everyone assumes that because you go to the Ice Academy, you're such a great skater. Well, I have news for them—I'm just as good as you and Carla, maybe even better."

Before Jill could respond, Carla walked over to them. She plunked her skate bag onto a seat next to Tori.

"Do you really think you're a better skater than Jill and me?" Carla demanded.

Tori's eyes flashed. "Who asked you to butt in?"

"Carla, no one is talking about who skates better—" Jill began.

"Oh, no? If you ask me, your good friend Tori is just plain old jealous of you," Carla said, a smile on her face.

"I am not jealous of Jill," Tori fired back. "I'm just being realistic."

Carla scoffed. Tori stared at her hard, then shook her head. She gathered her stuff and marched off to the locker room. Jill started to follow her, but Carla called her back.

"I'm right, you know, Jill. You are a better skater, especially since you've been training in Denver. *I'm* impressed. Tori is jealous, and she's always going to be jealous."

"You don't know what you are talking about, Carla," Jill retorted. "Tori's not jealous. She's just disappointed that she wasn't chosen to be a captain. That's all. So just back off, please? Tori will get over it."

6

July 14

Yo Morgan!

Aren't you surprised to get a letter from your big sister the very first week of camp?

You'd love it here at Redwood. There's a cool stable, and I'm going to check out the horses tomorrow.

Everything's going great, except for Jill. She's the one who used to skate with Silver Blades before going to the Ice Academy in Denver. I don't think she likes me. She got all bent out of shape after I pulled a funny joke on her. I like her; she's really cool and she's an awesome skater. I hope she changes her mind and lets me be friends with her. But it's no big deal if she doesn't. Tori and I get along great and we stick together.

I came up with a fantastic plan for tonight. The boys' camp is on the other side of the road from the girls' camp. Arleen Watson, the camp director, warned us the first night that the girls are not allowed in the boys' camp, and the boys are not allowed in the girls' camp. Breaking this rule means BIG trouble.

Of course, I can't resist. Tonight I'm going to wake up my friends, sneak over to the boys' camp with them, and raid Patrick's bunk. This is going to be so cool!

Love, Haley

"Hey, Jill. Wake Up. Come on, wake up."

"Huh? What?" Jill asked sleepily, her eyes still closed.

"You've got to get up. Now," Haley whispered.

Jill opened her eyes. Haley was reaching up to shake her awake. Jill sat up. Tori, Nikki, and Danielle were already up, getting dressed in the darkness of the bunk. "What time is it?" she whispered.

"Three in the morning," Haley whispered. "Time to go raid Alex and Patrick's bunk!" With that, Haley yanked Jill's blanket off her bed.

A few minutes later the five girls tiptoed out of their bunk and huddled together outside. The sky was still dark, and the grass was covered with the cold dew of early morning. Jill shivered and asked, "Whose crazy idea was this again?"

"Mine," Haley said with a pleased grin.

"What are we supposed to do now?" Tori asked. "It's cold out here."

"Yeah," Danielle agreed. "And if Merry catches us, I'm sure we're going to be in *big* trouble."

"She'll never know we're missing," Haley assured them. "I've got the perfect plan."

"What is it?" Nikki asked, jogging in place to keep warm. She was still wearing her pajamas.

"We sneak across the road to Patrick and Alex's bunk. And then we *decorate* it," Haley explained with a giggle.

"Decorate? What does that mean?" Jill asked.

Haley showed them the bundled-up sweatshirt she was carrying. She opened it up, and five rolls of toilet paper fell out.

"We're going to wrap their bunk in toilet paper!" Haley exclaimed mischievously. Jill, Danielle, Tori, and Nikki began to laugh as they each grabbed a roll.

"This is going to be fun," Jill said.

"Let's go!" Tori cried. She led the group toward the boys' bunks.

"Here it is," Haley whispered when they reached the redwood bunk with the number twelve on it. "This is Alex and Patrick's bunk."

"Alex has no idea what he's in for," Nikki said with a giggle.

It's nice to hear Nikki laugh, Jill thought. And Tori seems to have forgotten all about being captain. Haley sure has a knack for making people smile, Jill realized.

In the darkness the boys' bunks looked just like the girls'. Jill wondered which bunk Ross Barrett, the cute boy with the blond curls, was sleeping in.

"Okay," Haley commanded. "Tori, Dani, and I will wrap the bunk with toilet paper. Nikki, you decorate the nearby trees. Jill, you cover the porch."

"Excellent," Danielle said, pushing her hair out of her eyes. None of them had bothered to brush their hair, Jill realized. Luckily none of the boys would be awake to see them.

"We've got to work fast and get back to our bunk," Haley warned. "Let's go!"

Jill watched as Haley, Tori, and Danielle began wrapping toilet paper around Bunk Twelve. The boys were certainly going to be surprised in the morning, Jill thought with a smile.

Nikki twirled the toilet paper around the trees as if she were decorating them for Christmas. Jill set to work on the porch. She wove the white paper around the railing, careful to avoid the damp bathing suits that were drying there. She wrapped the small porch bench and when she was done, there was no wood in sight. Only white toilet paper.

"We're finished with the bunk," Haley whispered.

She stood with Tori and Danielle on the grass along-side the porch.

"I just finished the trees," Nikki said, joining them.

"Wait one second," Jill pleaded. "I'm almost done. I want to put some more on the railing."

But as Jill hurried to the opposite side of the porch, the floorboards let out a loud creak and groan.

"Who's out there?" a boy's voice called.

The five girls exchanged panicked looks. Haley put her finger to her lips, motioning for them to keep quiet.

Jill tried to tiptoe back across the porch, toward her friends. But at that moment a light went on inside the bunk.

"Hey, what gives!" a boy yelled as he pushed against the door. "We're trapped in here!"

Jill couldn't help but laugh. Then the boys pushed hard and broke the toilet-paper barrier.

"Run, Jill!" Danielle cried.

Jill leaped off the porch and ran toward her friends. She could hear Haley and Tori laughing as they crouched behind a large evergreen tree along-side Bunk Twelve.

"Hey, Haley, is that you out there?" Patrick called as he stood on the porch with a group of boys.

"It's definitely got to be Haley, Nikki, and crowd," Alex said. "You can run, but you can't hide! Just wait—we'll get you on the ice!"

"Oh, please," Haley groaned quietly. Jill giggled as she knelt beside her, out of breath.

"Look what they did to our bunk," said another boy.

Jill peered around the tree to see who was speaking. It was Ross Barrett—the cute boy from the parking lot! He was in Alex and Patrick's bunk. She couldn't believe it.

"Who's out there?" the boys' counselor demanded as he hurried onto the porch and peered into the darkness.

"I've got a plan," Jill whispered. They all huddled close. "We've got to get out of here without the boys and their counselor seeing us. I think we should sneak away, one by one, behind the bunk next door. There's a path that leads to the gravel road. If we're quiet, the boys won't see us."

Everyone nodded their agreement.

"I'll go first," Danielle volunteered as they heard Alex shout into the darkness, "Come out, come out, wherever you are!"

Each girl slowly left the safety of the tree and ran toward the girls' bunks. Danielle first, then Haley, Nikki, and Tori. Jill was the last one left. She crept out from behind the evergreen. Then she started to run.

"Look, it's one of the girls!"

Jill turned her head in the direction of the boy's voice. It was Ross! Panicking, she froze in her tracks. The two of them locked eyes, then Ross smiled and waved at her. Jill felt the color rise to her cheeks.

"It's Jill," Alex cried. She turned and bolted. "We're going to get you!" he yelled after her.

But Jill barely heard him. Instead, as she dashed to the safety of the girls' camp, all she could think was, I'm in love!

7

Dear Mom,

Hi! Camp is totally fun! But don't worry—I'm not slacking off. I'm practicing tons of hours a day. The coaches here are nice, but I don't think they're nearly as good as the Silver Blades coaches.

Now for the bad news. Carla Benson from Blade Runners is here. She's showing off, as usual, but I'm going to prove to her that I'm the better skater. Just wait until next winter's Regionals!

All the coaches seem to like me a lot. They wanted to make me captain of one of the color-war teams, but I decided to let Jill do it. I need the time to work on my skating. My goal is to land the double axel by

*the end of the summer. Everyone's sure I'll be able
to do it in time for the color war.*

*It's fun having Haley at camp with us—we're
always "buddies" for swim instruction! Can you
believe the waterfront counselor made me swim
four laps in the freezing-cold lake yesterday morning! Maybe you can call the camp and complain
about that.*

Please write. I love to get letters.
                                    Love, Tori

The morning after the girls raided the boys' camp, Jill
sat in the bleachers watching Nikki and Alex skate.
She held her breath as Alex spun Nikki around in
a difficult and dramatic move called a death spiral.
Nikki held her position perfectly, then came out of the
spin with a triumphant grin on her face. The couple
circled the rink, finishing their freestyle program with
a high-flying lift. When the music crashed to a halt,
Jill clapped until her hands hurt. "Wow, you guys are
amazing!"

Nikki's face was flushed from exertion when she
skated toward the bleachers.

"That's an awesome routine!" Jill cried enthusiasti-
cally. "Did Kathy arrange it for you?" Kathy Bart was
Nikki and Alex's Silver Blades skating coach. She was
very demanding, but Jill knew Kathy was one of the
reasons she'd made it all the way to the Academy.

Alex skated over to join them. He grinned while

rubbing a towel through his dark curly hair. "Boy, that was some workout," he said. "Especially since some of us have been awake since three o'clock this morning." He raised his eyebrows at Jill and Nikki. "Come on. Admit it was Bunk Nine who raided us. We saw you, anyway."

Jill wanted to ask if the boys' counselor had seen her too, but Nikki jumped in. "Never! You can't prove a thing."

"Just remember—when you least expect it, we're going to get you back," Alex warned them. "You're just lucky we didn't give Jason, our counselor, your names."

Whew! Jill thought, and she exchanged glances with Nikki.

Danielle, Tori, and Haley skated up to the barrier.

"We're going in for a shower," Danielle announced. "Are you coming, Nikki and Jill?"

"We'll be right there," Jill replied, holding Nikki's arm. Alex waved good-bye and headed off to the boys' locker room.

As soon as the other girls were out of earshot, Jill turned to her friend. "Nikki, I'm so excited about the baby. It's going to be so much fun. And anything you want to know about babies, I can tell you."

Nikki sighed. "Thanks, Jill. I don't know why this is bugging me so much. It just feels weird to become a sister at thirteen—"

"But it's great to be an older sister," Jill interrupted.

"It's so much fun playing with little kids. And teaching them stuff too."

"I know," Nikki agreed. "It's just not what I expected and—"

"But you've baby-sat before," Jill interrupted again. "It's just like that, only all the time."

"It's not playing with the baby that has me freaked. . . ." Nikki said, her voice trailing off.

"But, Nikki, it's so cool your mom is having a baby!" Jill tried to persuade her.

"Yeah, I guess," Nikki said softly. "Look, Jill, let's drop it, okay?"

Jill stared at Nikki. Didn't Nikki trust her anymore? Jill used to think she and Nikki were very close, but now . . .

Was it something Jill had done—or was it just that things between them had changed forever?

"We've been at camp only five days, and I've already made seven lanyard bracelets!" Tori complained that afternoon as the girls in Bunk Nine headed for their scheduled period in the arts and crafts shack. "By the end of the summer I won't have any more room on my arms to wear all the bracelets I make."

"So make something else," Haley suggested, opening the shack's door. The smell of turpentine wafted out. Nikki hurried inside ahead of the others. "Nikki and I are doing ceramics," Haley said.

"Clay is way too messy," Tori said, wrinkling her nose. "Besides Carla's doing ceramics, and I'm trying to stay away from her."

"I've got a great idea for a really cool project," Jill said suddenly.

"What is it?" Danielle asked.

"It has to be a secret from Nikki," Jill whispered.

All morning Jill had been thinking about her talk with her friend. Jill was determined to get Nikki to open up and trust her again. Maybe all Nikki needed was to see how much Jill and the others cared about her. And maybe they could help her to feel more excited about the baby's coming.

Tori, Danielle, and Haley gathered around Jill as she told them her idea. "Well, Nikki seems so bummed out since we got to camp. Why don't we make her a surprise present from all of us to cheer her up?"

"Jill, that's the greatest idea!" Danielle exclaimed. "You always come up with fantastic ideas. Remember when we couldn't think of a theme for last spring's ice show, and we had to call you all the way in Colorado to come to our rescue? You're the best when it comes to creative things."

"Shhh," Jill said, blushing at the praise. "Don't let Nikki hear us!"

"What should we make?" Tori asked.

"It would be neat to make a present for the new baby," Jill said, pausing a moment to think. "I've got it! We could make a wall hanging out of colored felt.

My littlest sister, Laurie, has the cutest one hanging in her room."

"I love it!" Danielle declared. "But what about Nikki? Our bunk always has arts and crafts together. How can we keep it a surprise from her?"

"Leave that to me," Haley replied mischievously. "You guys just get the supplies together, and I'll meet you at the back table in two minutes." Jill wondered what Haley had planned, as the younger girl walked over to Kit Marcus, the arts and crafts counselor, and began whispering in her ear.

A few minutes later Haley took a seat at their table. Suddenly Kit announced loudly, "Nikki, Carla, Sharon, and Sandy—I want to give you guys special instructions on how the ceramics kiln works. Let's all go downstairs where the kiln is. The rest of the bunk will work upstairs."

"Haley, you're a genius!" Tori declared as Nikki followed Kit and the other three girls downstairs. Kit winked at Haley before she left.

Haley smiled and said, "Let's get working. What kinds of shapes should we cut out of the felt?"

"How about baby animals?" Jill suggested.

"Not bad," Haley agreed. "But I think to make it perfect for Nikki, it would be great to put little felt ice skates on the animals!"

Danielle nodded, and Jill agreed that Haley had come up with a good idea. She took a pair of scissors and began to cut a baby bunny rabbit out of a piece of pink felt. As the four girls worked, Jill announced, "Right before lunch today Carla and I met with Robin, and we picked our color-war teams. I'm captain of the red team, and I picked all you guys to be on my team."

"I should hope so," Danielle said with a laugh. "I'd die if I had to be on Carla's team."

Tori didn't say anything.

"Robin gave me a list of the jumps and spins that I have to assign for next Saturday's skate-off," Jill continued. "I'm supposed to decide which girl is best at what, since the competition pits one red-team member against one yellow-team member for each move."

"That's a tough job," Haley observed, busily cutting a piece of bright orange felt.

Jill nodded. "I thought I'd start with my friends. You know, give you guys the good stuff and then give the rest of the team what's left over."

"Cool," Haley said, looking over Jill's shoulder at the typed list of skating moves. "Can I perform the split jump?"

"That would be great," Jill replied. "You're amazing at split jumps. Dani, how about if you take the camel-sitspin combination?"

"Sure, if that's what you want," Danielle agreed. "Anything for the red team."

Jill smiled and turned to Tori. "Tori, I thought you'd be great at the double-Lutz jump. Okay?"

Tori stared down at the table for a few moments. When she looked up at Jill, her face was red. "No, that's *not* okay," she said. "I want to do the double axel instead."

"But, Tori, you can't land a double axel yet," Jill reminded her. "I saw you try it during our lesson yesterday."

"And you think you're the only one around here who can do one?" Tori challenged. "I could land a double axel by next week if I had to."

"It's not worth taking that chance and losing the color war," Jill tried to explain. "Do the double Lutz instead, okay?"

"Well, I guess I have no choice. *You're* the captain. Robin gave you the power to tell me what to do," Tori said with a huff.

"Look, Tori," Jill began, "I—"

"Hey, you guys, check out the awesome felt animals Haley is making," Danielle called out suddenly, obviously trying to change the subject. "Giraffes and hippos and elephants in Day-Glo colors. We should all make funky animals like those."

"I agree," Tori said. "Haley's animals are much better than these stupid pastel bunnies and lambs Jill and I are cutting out."

Jill looked down at her little pile of felt animals and sighed. She liked her baby animals, but she didn't feel like making a big deal out of it, especially since Tori was already angry with her. She began to cut a lion out of hot-pink felt.

"It's so amazing that Haley is good at art and can come up with all these great ideas," Danielle said, her brown eyes sparkling. "Now we won't have to keep calling you in Colorado, Jill, and bothering you for ideas when we get stuck. We're so lucky—we have Haley now!"

Jill swallowed hard. "Yeah," she said softly. "I guess you are."

"**S**o, what's next on the schedule?" Nikki asked as the five girls left the arts and crafts shack together. Nikki still didn't know anything about the surprise wall hanging. Kit had let them hide it in the shack until they could finish it. "I can't get used to where we have to be when," Nikki said.

"You and the rest of us"—Haley made a face—"plus Carla, have a riding lesson in ten minutes. Jill, what do you, Sharon, and Sandy have?"

"Tennis," Jill answered. "But I'm really not in the mood for tennis."

"You could just not show up for tennis and come riding with us," Haley offered. "I'm sure Merry would love to have you join the group for the lesson."

Danielle chuckled. "Even if she agreed to cut tennis, Jill wouldn't go with us. She doesn't ride. Horses aren't her thing."

"Oh?" Haley said.

"As in she *detests* them," Tori explained.

Jill frowned. "I wouldn't say *that*."

Haley looked at her watch. "We'd better get going. We have to groom and curry the horses first, and Merry's been pretty rough on us if our tack isn't polished."

The four of them hurried to the stable. As she watched their backs, Jill let out a long sigh. Why do I always feel left out? I thought Nikki, Danielle, and Tori were my best friends, and now they've totally replaced me with Haley! Brushing away tears, Jill decided that she wasn't going to her scheduled tennis lesson after all. She headed for the ice rink instead. Jill didn't care if the tennis counselor yelled at her. When she felt sad, she knew the best way to cheer herself up was to skate.

Ten minutes later Jill was circling the rink backward, her strong legs pushing into each stroke. She went into a layback spin, twirling rapidly over the gleaming ice. Then she straightened out and began practicing her jumps. She was so caught up in the movements, she didn't notice the other skater until he was right behind her.

"Excellent double toe loop."

Jill whirled around, and found herself gazing into a pair of pure blue eyes. They belonged to Ross Barrett, who was grinning at her. "We meet again."

"Thanks," Jill mumbled. "I—uh—have to tighten my skate laces." She skated over to the bleachers alongside the rink.

Ross stayed right behind her. "My name's Ross Barrett," he said, dropping down onto one of the benches.

"Uh . . . I'm Jill, Jill Wong," she mumbled.

"I know. We sort of met last night," Ross replied with a grin. "After you and your friends covered our bunk with toilet paper."

Jill blushed. An embarrassed silence hung over them. Jill didn't know what to say next.

"Where are you from?" Jill asked shyly.

"Montana," Ross replied. "Bozeman, Montana. How about you?"

"I'm really from Pennsylvania, but right now I'm living in Denver."

"Are you at the Ice Academy?"

Jill nodded. "I've been there since March."

"Wow, you must be a good skater." Ross sounded impressed. "Show me your routine."

"Okay," Jill said before she knew what she was saying. She stepped back onto the ice, while Ross leaned back against the bleachers and gave her the thumbs-up sign.

Jill blushed again and skated toward the center of the ice rink. It made her nervous to perform for someone she liked. There were only a few campers using the other end, so Jill had almost the whole rink to herself. She popped her music into the tape deck, and sounds of the newest Whitney Houston song filled the arena.

Jill decided to skate the part of her routine that she had performed at the last Ice Academy show. She took a deep breath and raised her arms in the air. Posing for a second or two, she then skated forward and went right into a camel spin. As the beat of the music filled her head, her embarrassment disappeared. She was enjoying herself and was really glad that she had skipped tennis.

She completed several split jumps, an axel–double toe loop combination, a flying sitspin, and ended with her double axel. Her face was flushed with excitement as she finished her routine. Ross was smiling and clapping loudly.

"Great!" he called out as she skated to the edge of the rink.

"Thanks," Jill said. "Now it's your turn."

"Uh-uh. Not after that routine. No way am I going to fall on my face in front of you."

"Not fair," Jill protested. "I want to see you skate."

"Okay." Ross stepped onto the ice. "You asked for it, but don't be surprised if I crash and burn!"

The music was still playing the same lively beat, and Jill sat back on the bleachers, wondering how good a skater he really was. She wasn't disappointed. Ross was good. His skating was polished, strong, and very graceful. His jumps and spins left her almost breathless. He was definitely good enough to train at the Ice Academy. Jill found herself thinking back to the campfire and the unusual wish he had made. She wondered if he had any plans or dreams for a skating career.

Ross ended his performance with a double axel, just as she had. Jill clapped and cheered.

As he skated up to the railing, the music changed to a slow-dance tune. "Wanna dance?" he drawled.

"Now? Here?" Jill didn't know how to respond.

"Yeah, why not? Ice dancing."

"I can't, ummm, dance . . . on the ice, I mean." Her voice trailed off.

"You can skate on the ice, right?" Ross asked in a teasing tone.

Jill nodded.

"And you like to dance?"

"Sure."

"So," he teased, "come on. It's easy. I'll show you."

Jill joined him on the ice. He put one arm around her back and held her hand with the other. Then he gently pushed her backward. "Just do the opposite of what I do," he told her.

Jill looked down at her feet and promptly slipped a little. She giggled. Ross cracked up. This time they both slipped and struggled.

"Okay, let's try again," Ross said encouragingly. "I know you'll get the hang of it."

"I've never tried ice dancing before," Jill admitted.

"I love it, but I'm only a beginner," Ross told her as they circled the rink together.

After a few minutes Jill began to catch the rhythm

of the music and was able to match it to her steps on the ice. With Ross's arms and hands guiding her, she completed several basic ice-dancing movements. It was great fun, and she wished they could dance together all afternoon.

Finally they decided to call it quits when the music changed to a military marching song.

"I remember your wish at the campfire. Are you really serious about skating?" Jill asked as she took off her skates.

Ross paused before answering. "I think I am," he admitted. "But sometimes I'm not sure. Part of me wants to hang around my uncle's ranch. Part of me just wants to skate. I don't talk much about skating when I'm at the ranch. The other guys there think it's kind of stupid. They're all cowboys—you know, rough-and-ready types. They don't go much for dancing and stuff like that."

"But you do," Jill said seriously. "And you're very good."

"Thanks," Ross replied. "I guess I'll have to get serious about skating, or else give it up."

"Why can't you just skate for fun?" Jill asked him.

"I can," Ross said, "but for me, it's more fun when I'm competing."

Then he told her that he had come to Redwood Skating Camp because it was the only camp that combined both skating and horseback riding.

"I guess you like to ride," Jill said quietly. Another

horseback rider, she was thinking. She wished he'd said he liked to swim, or even rollerblade.

Ross nodded. "You bet. I could ride before I could walk." He looked at her with a shy grin. "Hey, I've got a great idea."

"What?" Jill asked, almost afraid of what was coming next.

"Let's go riding together."

"Oh." Jill tried to hide her disappointment. Would Ross lose interest in her if she admitted to being hopeless around horses?

"How about next Sunday? Everyone has a free period then." Ross didn't seem to notice that she wasn't very excited.

"Ummm . . ." Jill stalled for time to think. She bent over to unlace her skates. "Riding . . . next Sunday." She took a deep breath. "Sure, why not?" She couldn't believe what she'd just agreed to. She'd never been on a horse before!

"Great," Ross said happily. "I've already checked out the trails, and there's a terrific waterfall about an hour's ride into the woods. Okay?"

Again Jill hesitated.

"Well?" he asked. And then he said, "If you're busy, we could always go some other time."

"No," Jill said quickly. "It's fine, it's just that, well, I'm really not that great with horses." She looked away from him and picked up her skating boots. *I've probably blown my chances,* she said to herself.

"That's no problem," she heard Ross say. "We'll just take it easy. Don't worry, I'm a real pro on horseback. Trust me. I'll pick a real easy trail and I'll give you some lessons before we go."

"Okay," Jill agreed slowly. Then she grinned. "I learn fast." She picked up her skating bag and walked with him to the door.

"See you at ten o'clock next Sunday morning," Ross said, before jogging off toward the boys' bunks.

"Right," Jill called after him. Now she'd really done it. How on earth was she going to go on a trail ride with him and not look like a fool?

She walked back to her bunk, her mind racing through all the possibilities. Well, no matter what it takes, Jill vowed to herself, I'm going to get over my fear of horses. And I'm going to do it this week.

9

July 15

Dear Kyle,

Hi! How's summer in Seneca Hills? I REALLY miss you! Thanks for answering my first letter so fast. I've read your letter five times already. Working at the snack bar at the community pool sounds like a riot—I loved the story of how the blender went out of control when you were making milk shakes. Every time I think of you covered with chocolate ice cream, I burst out laughing!

Camp is really busy. When I'm not skating, I'm swimming or playing softball. It's nice to have the whole group together again. But it's kind of weird to see how many things change in just a few months—

like Haley and Tori becoming best friends. And Jill's done lots of new things in Colorado—she even learned how to ride a horse there! And then there's me becoming an older sister. . . .

In your letter you said you were really surprised to hear that my mom was going to have a baby. It's weird, huh? I haven't been too excited about the baby. It's hard to get used to the idea of not being the only child anymore. And everything has been so great since we moved to Seneca Hills—I wish it could all stay the same forever. I told my friends about Mom being pregnant. They're so happy about baby-sitting and all that, that they never give me a chance to explain how I freaked out I am.

And my parents haven't been a big help either. Can you believe that I've been here almost a week and the only mail I've gotten from them is one lousy postcard? I guess they've been really busy getting ready for the baby. But Jill's family has sent her five letters already!!! And of course you wrote me a GREAT letter!

Okay, I guess I've done enough complaining. Sorry, but you're the only one who hasn't made a really big deal over the baby, so I thought you'd understand how confused I am over it. I wish I could see you in person—I miss you! A LOT!

I've got to go now—the bell is ringing for dinner. Please write back!

Love, Nikki

"Hey, Jill!" Danielle shouted over the noise of the dining hall that evening.

"I think she's deaf!" Haley declared, reaching across Jill's plate for the salt. "She must have cotton in her ears."

"What?" Jill looked up guiltily. She had been so busy thinking about Ross that she hadn't heard a word anybody said.

Danielle groaned. "For the *fourth* time, please pass the ketchup."

Jill reached across the table and passed the sticky bottle to Danielle. Jill was dying to tell her friends about Ross. She'd been holding in the good news all afternoon, waiting for the right moment to tell everyone at the same time. She glanced across the table at Carla, Sandy, and Sharon and wondered if she should wait until they left. No, Jill decided, this news is too exciting to keep secret. But just as she was ready to tell everyone, Danielle started speaking.

"Nikki, have you heard from home? How's your mom?"

Nikki managed a weak smile. "I got a postcard a couple of days ago. She's okay."

"When's the baby due?" Tori asked.

Jill joined in. "Yeah, Nikki, you haven't told us *when* you're going to be a big sister."

"Six months." Nikki didn't look up.

"I think it's really exciting," Danielle declared. "I wish I had a sister."

"Why not another brother?" Haley asked.

Danielle buried her head in her arms and let out a huge groan.

Tori nudged Danielle and laughed. "Nicholas isn't that bad!"

"Sure, if you like living with half the local hockey team."

"Sounds pretty good to me." Haley grinned.

Danielle shook her head. "It's awful. Trust me. I can never get in the bathroom, his dirty clothes are everywhere, I'm always falling over his hockey sticks, and he lives on the phone! Mom's about ready to make him pay for his own line. I'd swap him for a kid sister any day!"

"Hey, I hate to interrupt, but you guys won't believe the great thing that happened to me today!" Jill exclaimed, unable to wait any longer.

"What?" Danielle asked, leaning forward in her chair.

"Can you wait a second, Jill? I'm dying of thirst. I'm going to get a lemonade," Haley said.

"Sure, no problem," Jill said.

Haley stood up and looked at the rest of the group. "Anybody want anything while I'm up there?"

Carla poked her plate in front of Haley as she passed. "Since you asked . . ." She gave Haley her sweetest smile. "How about more mashed potatoes?"

"Right," Haley agreed, taking Carla's plate. "No problem. I'll just be a minute."

Haley returned a few minutes later holding Carla's plate and her own lemonade.

"Here," she said as she put Carla's plate in front of her. "You're in luck. These mashed potatoes are really fresh. A new batch."

Carla looked down. "Yum! I love when they're this creamy!" she grinned and licked her lips. "Extra gravy too! Thanks!"

Carla eagerly shoveled a large forkful of mashed potatoes into her mouth. "Yugh! What's this!" she choked, sending a spray of potatoes across the table. "These aren't mashed potatoes!"

Carla pushed her plate away, and it fell onto the floor. Gravy splattered everywhere.

"That's disgusting!" Tori cried. She stared at Carla. "What's wrong with you anyway?"

"Those potatoes are really weird," Carla said, shaking her head. "They taste like . . ."

"Whipped cream," Haley supplied sweetly. "I owed you one, Carla—for making me take the blame for short-sheeting Merry's bed."

Tori, Danielle, and Nikki began to laugh at Haley's joke.

"That really wasn't nice, Haley," Jill said, handing Carla some napkins. "In fact, it was kind of stupid."

Haley just stared at Jill.

"Gimme a break," Tori broke in as Jill watched Sharon help Carla clean off her beige shirt. "I can't believe you're taking this so seriously. It was just whipped cream."

"I know." Jill felt her face turn red. "And I'm not taking it seriously. I just think that sometimes Haley's jokes are kind of babyish. That's all."

"Oh, I see. Now that you've moved to Colorado, you think you're so much more grown-up than the rest of us, Jill," Tori replied. "I guess since we all laughed, that makes us babies too. Huh?"

"No, Tori, that's not what I meant." Jill didn't want to make such a big thing out of this and get into some kind of fight with Tori. Still Haley had to realize that not everyone found her jokes funny.

Haley cleared her throat. "Jill's right. It was a stupid joke. But when I saw that bowl of whipped cream, I just couldn't resist taking some."

"It's no big deal, Jill. I can take a joke," Carla said. And with that, Carla turned her back to them and began whispering to Sharon and Sandy.

"Hey," Danielle said suddenly. "Jill never got to tell us her big news. Come on, Jill, tell us."

Jill hesitated, but brightened at the thought of Ross. "Well," she started. "Guess who I met today?" A silly grin spread across her face. She glanced to the boys' side of the dining room but couldn't find Ross. "I sort of ran into him on the ice this afternoon."

Danielle's huge brown eyes widened.

"You mean the guy with the cowboy hat . . . the Nashville escapee!" Tori said, and smirked.

Danielle batted Tori with her napkin. "He's cute, Tori. Admit it. Just not your type."

"I have no type," Tori said, sounding superior. "I don't have time for boys, just skating."

"Well, la-di-da," Danielle teased.

"What were you doing at the rink, Jill?" Haley asked.

"I skipped tennis to skate," Jill explained.

"So—did you talk to him?" Nikki asked eagerly.

"Yes!" Jill exclaimed. "And guess what—we have a date next Sunday!"

Whooping with delight, Danielle shrieked loudly, "That's great, Jill!"

"So, where are you guys going on your date?" Tori asked.

"Um, we're going . . . riding," Jill admitted.

"You! On a horse!" Tori was shocked. "Jill, you've *never* been on a horse in your life. You'll break your neck . . . and everything else. . . ."

Jill rolled her eyes. "You sound like my mother, Tori," she said. "Really, it's not *that* big a deal."

"It is, Jill," Tori continued. "This guy is not worth falling off a horse and hurting yourself. One fall and your skating career is down the drain. Besides, you're just going to make a fool out of yourself if you go riding with him. Cancel the date. Now!"

Before Jill could stop herself, she turned to her friend. "Look, Tori, you don't know that for a fact . . . I mean, that I've never been on a horse before. . . ."

"But when we were all heading for the stables today, Dani said you couldn't ride," Haley reminded her.

"Yeah, that's right," Tori added. "Besides, I've known you for years. I know you can't ride."

"Well, as it happens, I *can* ride," Jill lied. "Not well . . ." she added quickly, crossing her fingers under the table. She *hated* lying. Her mother could always tell. The tips of her ears turned red. Luckily Jill had her hair down today, so none of her friends would notice. Besides, she was sick of Tori's being competitive and arguing with her. It was time to put her in her place. "But I've done *lots* of things you don't know about since I went to the Ice Academy."

"Oh really," Tori said. She raised her eyebrows.

"Yes," Jill went on, growing more confident by the moment. "I've been on two trail rides in Denver. I'm not very good at it, and I still don't *like* horses. But Ross is going to give me lessons." There, that ought to get them to leave me alone, she thought.

"But why didn't you tell me you knew how to ride?" Danielle sounded hurt.

"I didn't think about it," Jill said nonchalantly. "Besides I didn't say I *like* riding. I'd skip it completely . . . if . . ."

"If it weren't for Ross!" Nikki and Haley chanted together and started to giggle.

Jill joined in their laughter, even though inside she wanted to cry. Right before dinner she'd decided to ask Tori to help her learn how to ride. But that wasn't an option anymore—and neither was asking any of her other friends.

Uh-oh, she thought. If the Silver Blades girls couldn't help her, what was she going to do? Who could she possibly find now to teach her how to ride?

10

Dear Bronya,

You'll never guess what's happened to your room-mate from the Ice Academy—I've just met the most wonderful guy. And I, Jill Wong, have a date with him next Sunday!!!

That's the good news. The problem is he's invited me to go trail riding, and I'm scared to death. He has no idea that I'm totally stupid around horses. I need some serious help. I've never even sat on a horse before! Haley and Tori know how to ride, and I was going to ask them to give me a crash (!!) course. Except I'm not sure I trust Haley exactly— she plays lots of practical jokes and I'm afraid she'll stick a tack or whoopee cushion under my saddle.

*I am not kidding about this. And Tori . . . well, this
probably isn't the best time to ask her any favors.
I was made captain of the red team in the camp
color war, and she wasn't. Now she's mad at me.
I need help from someone, somewhere FAST.*

*Wish me luck, and please write. I might have a
couple of broken bones by the time you get this
letter, but Ross may be worth it. I wish you could
see this guy—he's soooo cute!*

Your friend, Jill

"Oh, hi, Carla," Jill said, entering the skating-rink locker room late the next morning. "What are you doing
here?"

"Robin scheduled an extra private lesson for me in
five minutes," Carla answered as she pulled a cream-
colored skating sweater out of her open locker.

"I just finished a special lesson with Robin too," Jill
said. "I had to miss windsurfing with our bunk. Was
it fun?"

"Yeah, but it was hard. Nobody but Haley could get
very far on the lake without falling over," Carla said,
tying her long blond hair into a ponytail. "Hey, I saw
the end of your lesson when I came in. You've really
mastered that triple toe loop–double salchow combination. You looked terrific out there today. I mean it.
I'm going to have a tough time beating you in the color
war." Then she smiled. For once it seemed sincere.

"Thanks, Carla," Jill said with a grin. "Your skating is really strong too."

Jill quickly changed into black shorts, a yellow tank top, and her sneakers. Her bunk had soccer as their next activity.

"You look really nice in yellow," Carla commented. Jill smiled. "Thanks."

"Hey, I couldn't help but hear you talking last night at dinner," Carla said, pulling up her skating tights. "Do you really have a date with that cute boy, Ross?"

Jill couldn't help herself. She smiled, and said, "Yeah. We've got a date to go horseback riding next Sunday."

"That's awesome!" Carla exclaimed. "I heard you putting Tori in her place last night too. It's great you learned to ride in Denver. Aren't horses the best?"

"Well . . ." Jill's voice trailed off as she glanced at her reflection in the mirror and brushed her hair. Why had she told her friends such a big lie?

"Is something wrong?" Carla asked.

"I can't ride," Jill blurted. Somehow saying it out loud made her feel a little better. She sat down on the bench and looked up at Carla and confessed. "I made up that story about riding in Denver because Tori made me so angry."

Carla's pale eyebrows arched up. "So, do something else. Play tennis instead." She picked up her bag and slung it over her shoulder.

"Uh-uh." Jill shook her head. "It's all settled. Ross is going to give me a quick riding lesson before we go on the trails. And I was dumb enough to tell him I was a fast learner." Jill paused, and then added, "I wish I'd never agreed to go riding with him. I'm scared to death!"

She shoved her brush in her bag. "And I can't take riding class when everyone else does either. Not now. It's too late. I already told everyone I know how to ride."

Carla looked directly at Jill. "Would you like me to help you?" she volunteered.

Jill stared at her in amazement. "You? Help *me*?"

"Sure. Why not. It sounds like you need some serious help. I could give you a few riding lessons so you won't embarrass yourself in front of Ross."

"Would Merry let you give me lessons?" Jill asked, still not quite convinced Carla wasn't up to some weird sort of trick.

"Sure. I've been riding since I was five. Merry knows that. She's been letting me help with the younger kids whenever I get a chance to drop by the stables. I give them lessons in the ring when she's too busy and when I can squeeze in the time. I love horses.

"How about tomorrow?" Carla went on quickly. "We can meet at the stables tomorrow at two-thirty. Our bunk has a free period then, and I was going down to the stables anyway to help Merry with the horses."

"Okay," Jill said finally. "Thanks." She felt awkward about accepting Carla's help, but the other girl's offer seemed genuine. Besides, hadn't Jill been telling her friends that it was important to set aside some of their earlier competitiveness?

Jill smiled at Carla. "You won't tell anyone else about this? I want to surprise the others."

"Sure," Carla replied. "I won't say a word. I promise. See you tomorrow." She smiled back, then left the locker room, just as Nikki, Danielle, Tori, and Haley entered.

"What are you guys doing here?" Jill asked her friends.

"We decided to stop by the rink and pick you up on our way to soccer," Danielle answered. "Are you ready? We don't want to be late."

"Thanks." Jill zipped her skating bag closed and followed them out of the locker room. Her head was still spinning from her conversation with Carla.

Jill found herself only half listening to Haley and Tori's stories of windsurfing as they trudged across the camp grounds. The soccer field was at the far end of the camp, right by the stables and the volleyball court.

"Oh, no! Look!" Danielle's horrified cry forced Jill out of her daydreams. She glanced in the direction that Danielle was pointing, and gasped.

"Is that what I think it is?" Jill could barely get the words out of her mouth.

"We are in *big* trouble!" Haley shouted as all five girls sprinted toward the volleyball court.

There sat Merry's bed, still made neatly, next to her wooden night table, complete with the paperback book she was reading, some stationery, a pen, and her box of tissues. The sign COUNSELOR'S TURF—KEEP

OUT, with Merry's name scribbled in black marker, was hanging from the volleyball net. And several articles of her clothing were draped over the net too!

"Who did this?" Jill exclaimed, unable to stop staring.

"Check out the other side of the volleyball court," Haley replied, shaking her head in disbelief. "I see something on the ground."

Jill peeked around the net and began to giggle. On the opposite side of the court, the word *REVENGE* was spelled out in strips of toilet paper on the ground.

"Alex!" Nikki cried. "He warned me that his bunk planned to get us back for the toilet-paper raid."

They all burst into giggles, until Danielle broke the mood. "You guys are missing something," she said. "You know how Merry hates having anyone touch her stuff. If she finds her things on display on the volleyball court, we're going to have *a lot* of explaining to do."

"And look!" Nikki pointed in the direction they had just come from. "The girls from Bunk Three are headed this way. They probably have volleyball now!"

"We've got to get Merry's stuff back in our bunk—*now!*" Jill cried. She frantically began pulling Merry's clothing off the net.

"But we'll be late for soccer," Tori protested.

"Think about it, Tori. Would you rather be late for soccer or have Arleen Watson call your mother and tell her you've been breaking camp rules?" Danielle reasoned.

"Yikes," Tori agreed. "You're right. Let's move!"

"Hurry!" Haley exclaimed as she and Danielle grabbed the ends of the bed and tried to jog toward their bunk with it. They kept tripping.

"Don't get grass stains on her blankets," Nikki warned, as she panted under the weight of Merry's night table. "Hey, Tori, don't forget the sign and the toilet paper!"

Jill quickly scanned the court to make sure they had everything. She scooped a stray sock off the grass and followed her friends back to the bunk, all the while trying not to completely wrinkle Merry's wardrobe.

Once in the bunk they hurried about frantically, replacing all of Merry's furniture and hanging all her clothes in the closet.

"Is this where it was before?" Jill asked as she taped Merry's sign back over her bed.

"Yes." Nikki collapsed alongside Tori and Danielle on her lower bunk. A moment later Jill and Haley threw themselves on Nikki's bed too.

"I can't believe those guys got us back for the toilet-paper raid," Haley said. "What sneaks!"

"I told Alex a couple of days ago how uptight Merry was about her things. He knew the best way to get us in the most trouble," Nikki replied.

"But we showed them. Merry will never know!" Danielle cried.

"She will if we get in trouble for missing soccer," Tori reminded them.

"Soccer?" Jill groaned, exhausted. "Sprinting across

the camp with Merry's clothes and bed was enough exercise, don't you think?"

"Hey, Jill, maybe we found a new Olympic sport for you—track and field and redecorating!" Danielle teased. And with that, all five girls began laughing.

11

Dear Renee,

Well, dear sister, I hope you appreciate this letter.
I am breaking some sort of stupid camp rule by
writing you after lights-off. How? you may ask.
With my flashlight under the covers.

Bunking with the girls from Silver Blades has
been a lot better than I thought. Believe it or not,
I think Jill Wong wants to be my friend. Can you
imagine? I must admit I sort of like her too. Jill
actually complimented my skating the other day—
I'm not kidding. And she stuck up for me in front
of her friends when this girl Haley played a really
dumb joke on me. Anyway, I'm teaching her how
to ride a horse this week. She wanted me to teach

*her, not Tori! Who knows—it looks like Jill may
dump those Silver Blades girls after all and hang
out with me now. If I get off the waiting list and
into the Academy, maybe we could room together.*

*Let me know how summer's going in Vermont.
And let me know immediately if I get any mail from
the Ice Academy!!*

Love, Carla

As Jill skated around the ice rink the next afternoon,
she glanced at the clock on the wall. It was two-fifteen.
Almost time to meet Carla at the stables. Jill had decided to go directly to the stables from the rink, without
stopping back at the bunk. She didn't want to explain
to her friends where she was going.

Jill took a deep breath, then raced off to the locker
room. There was no time for a shower, but it didn't
really matter. She'd probably get all hot and sticky
anyway down at the stables.

Carla was already there when Jill arrived. "Good,
you made it," she said as Jill walked into the tack
room.

"Is everything okay?" Jill asked nervously. "I mean,
did Merry say it would be all right for me to ride?"

"Sure," Carla replied as she picked up a hoofpick and
a couple of brushes. She handed one of the brushes to
Jill. "Let's go and brush your horse. We can talk while
we work."

As they went down the aisle that ran down the middle of the horse stalls, Merry Walker entered the barn. "Oh, there you are, Carla," she said as she walked toward the two girls. "I see you're getting ready for Jill's lesson."

Merry tugged Jill's braid gently. "I'm glad you decided to try riding. Horses *can* be fun. I'm sorry that I'm too busy to look out for you myself; I have a trail ride to take out in ten minutes," she said. "But Carla's a good teacher. She's been helping with the beginners." She turned to Carla. "You're putting her on Smokey?"

"Right," Carla replied.

"He's quiet enough for a beginner. Just go easy for the first lesson," Merry cautioned.

As Merry headed off toward the tack room, Jill followed Carla to the end of the barn. Jill hesitated before the door, took a deep breath, and went into the stall.

"This is Smokey," Carla said cheerfully as she ran the brush over the black horse's back. "Why don't you go on the other side of him and brush his mane." Noticing Jill's slight hesitation, she added, "He's as gentle as a lamb. He won't bite!"

Reassured, Jill got to work untangling the horse's thick black mane. On his other side Carla had finished brushing his coat and was now busy cleaning out his hooves with the hoofpick.

A while later, as she showed Jill how to bridle and saddle the horse, she asked Jill what it was like to skate at the Ice Academy.

"I love it," Jill replied. She kept her eyes on Smokey as she talked. Every time Smokey stomped a hoof or snorted, she jumped a little. "At first, though, getting used to the place was really tough. I didn't know anyone, and I felt like my coaches were pushing me too hard."

"I guess they have to." Carla sounded sympathetic. Carla led the horse out of the barn and into the riding ring.

"Okay, Jill, this is it. Are you ready?"

Jill nodded. She took a deep breath and tried desperately not to let her terror show. She had made up her mind she was going to learn to ride. And once Jill Wong made up her mind about something, a herd of wild horses couldn't keep her from it. But today the thought of wild horses made her knees knock.

Carla showed her how to mount, and after a couple of false starts Jill swung herself into the saddle and instantly clutched Smokey's black mane.

Jill made herself look down. The ground seemed awfully far away.

"Don't hold on to his mane," Carla instructed. She took Jill's hands and made her hold the reins. "This is the right position," she told her. She showed Jill how to squeeze the horse's sides with her legs to urge him forward into a walk.

When Jill tried it, sure enough, Smokey responded to the pressure of her strong skater's legs.

"That's it," Carla encouraged. "Sit up straight, and keep your hands still."

"My hands aren't the problem," Jill cried. "It's my knees. My legs are shaking. That won't make him go faster, will it?"

Carla threw her head back and laughed. "No way, Jill."

After fifteen minutes of walking around the ring, with Carla standing in the center calling out instructions and encouragement, Jill began to relax. She still felt awkward, but not as bad as when she'd first gotten into the saddle.

"I think you're ready to start trotting now," Carla yelled out.

"Uh-uh," Jill protested. "Can't I just walk?"

"Not if you want to go riding with Ross," Carla replied. "He won't want to walk all the time, and anyway he'll expect you to know more than this." She then explained what Jill had to do when the horse began to trot.

Jill sighed. "Okay, I'm ready."

Trotting was a whole lot different from just walking. Jill bobbed around in the saddle, feeling like a toy ship being bounced on top of a tidal wave. It was awful, and she wanted to stop.

"You're doing great!" Carla cried.

Jill didn't agree with her. She felt as if every bone in her body had suddenly come loose, and she had no control over what was happening. Fortunately the horse appeared to tire of her flopping around on his back, because he slowed to a walk.

Jill heaved a sigh of relief and relaxed in the saddle.

"If I can somehow convince Ross that it's more fun to walk than trot, I'll have no trouble on our date."

"Don't worry, you'll get the hang of it," Carla said. Then she suggested that they take a break to cool off.

Jill dismounted stiffly, and they tethered Smokey to one of the ring's wooden posts. As they settled themselves under a grove of trees, Jill admitted, "It's harder than I thought it would be."

"The first lesson is always the toughest," Carla told her. "But you won't have any trouble. You're a terrific athlete, and your legs are strong."

Jill smiled. "Thanks, Carla."

"It would be great if I'm chosen to go to the Ice Academy next year," Carla said. "Then we could hang out together."

"That would be fun," Jill agreed, smiling at Carla.

"Ross is really cute," Carla went on. "He kind of reminds me of my boyfriend, Ted. You know, the outdoor type. You must be real excited about your date."

"Yeah, and nervous too," Jill admitted.

"Don't sweat it!" Carla grinned. "You'll do fine. Hey, let's get going again. You've got more to learn."

Jill untied the horse and clambered back into the saddle.

"Okay, now walk around the ring once and then start trotting," Carla instructed as she positioned herself in the center of the ring.

After one circle Jill began to trot. This time it didn't feel quite as uncomfortable, and Carla yelled, "You've got it! That's right. Keep going."

Jill started to smile. Maybe I won't fall flat on my face in front of Ross after all, she thought.

"Jill, that was fantastic!" Carla cried when Jill trotted up to her. "I can't believe how well you're doing!" Jill got off the horse and to her surprise Carla hugged her.

If Tori could see me now! Jill thought, then awkwardly hugged Carla back.

As they headed to the barn to put Smokey back in his stall, Jill realized she'd really enjoyed the afternoon. Carla had been fun to hang out with and very generous with her time. Jill had misjudged Carla and so had her friends.

From now on, Jill decided, I'm going out of my way to be nice to Carla Benson.

12

July 20

Dear Grandma,

Skating, camp, and everything are perfect . . . well—almost perfect. Jill seems so different. She's much more serious than she used to be. And the new Jill is an even better skater than she was back at Silver Blades. She's a lot better than us, and Tori is jealous of course. The weirdest thing is the way Jill's suddenly spending all this time with Carla Benson. (Remember Carla—the Blade Runners' queen of mean?) Nikki and Tori haven't noticed, and I haven't said anything, but Jill and Carla are up to something. And I think I know what it is!

The other news is that Nikki's mom is going to have a baby. Isn't that neat? Nikki has been really *freaked out about it. Today we gave her this goofy wall hanging we made for over the crib. We thought it would be a great surprise, but it made Nikki cry. I guess this next year isn't going to be easy for Nikki. I'm going to try to help—I told her she could sleep over at our house every Friday night. That's okay, isn't it?*

I miss all of you, but especially your baking, Grandma. Please send us something wonderful to eat. Make sure there's enough of it to go around Bunk Nine.

All my love, Dani

"Jill Wong!" Robin Turner shouted across the rink three days later. "You can do better than that!" Jill cringed when she heard the anger in the usually mild-mannered coach's voice. "Try that double toe loop again!"

Jill grit her teeth and tried to ignore the awful aches in her thighs. She had never truly appreciated the term *saddle sore* before.

Determined to do better, Jill worked up the momentum she needed for the jump. But as she took off from the surface of the ice, she felt her legs go weak and wobble.

Crash! That was the third time she'd fallen in the last half hour. Jill sat up, brushed the ice chips off her tights, and struggled to her feet. Her legs were so stiff from riding that she wasn't surprised she had barely landed one jump.

Jill winced. "Sorry, Robin. I'll try it again."

The jump wasn't particularly difficult. In fact Jill had landed it many times. She could even land a triple! However, that was before she'd started riding. She'd had three more lessons with Carla over the past few days, and she was getting a little discouraged. Even though Carla praised everything she did, Jill still felt scared whenever she was riding Smokey. Would she really be ready to go on a long trail ride with Ross?

This time around the rink Jill gathered speed and lifted into the air, managing to do two complete revolutions before she landed. She didn't fall, but she knew that the landing could have been much better. The color war was only four days away, and Jill was worried. If her legs were still stiff for the competition, she certainly wouldn't be able to land her double axel. And then, she knew, Tori would never let her hear the end of it. Tori was still annoyed that Jill wouldn't let her perform the double axel.

"I guess that's all for now," Robin said as she skated up to Jill. "You're still missing that landing. Is anything wrong?"

"No, everything's fine," Jill said quickly. "I'm a little tired today, that's all."

"See you tomorrow, then," Robin said, and she skated off toward her next group of students.

Just then Ross skated by. Jill turned and looked at him. He caught her glance and winked at her. Jill smiled at him, suddenly glad all over again that she was learning to ride.

"I saw that wink."

Jill jumped, then turned around. Danielle was standing right behind her, grinning widely.

"He's really cute," Danielle said, staring at Ross. He was at the other end of the arena, talking to his coach. "Even without that neat cowboy hat he wears."

"I know," Jill agreed. "I'm going to take my skates off," she told Danielle, and skated toward the bleachers.

Danielle followed her, but stayed on the ice. She leaned against the boards and watched as Jill sat down and started to remove her skates.

"So what's new?" Danielle asked.

Jill tugged at her laces and looked up. Danielle was trying very hard to look casual. "New?" Jill repeated cautiously.

"Yeah. Have you been doing anything new lately?" Danielle pressed.

"Dani, what are you talking about? What would I be doing that's *new*?" Jill asked, wondering exactly what Danielle was fishing for.

"Learning to ride," Danielle said.

Jill's mouth fell open. She certainly hadn't told any of her friends about Carla.

"How did you . . . I mean, who told . . . ?" Jill trailed off.

"I overheard Sharon and Sandy talking about it. I was sitting near them at the lake yesterday."

"Sandy and Sharon!" Jill repeated, shocked. Carla had *promised* not to tell *anyone*.

"Come on," Danielle urged. "Spill the beans about you and Carla. What's going on?"

"She's just helping me with my riding, that's all," Jill said. She bent down and slipped her feet into her sneakers.

"Bad move," Danielle replied. "You're crazy to hang out with her. You know what she's like."

"You're wrong," Jill said firmly. "She's a very nice person."

"I don't trust her, Jill. Why are you letting her help you? If you need riding lessons, and you won't ask Tori, why not ask Merry, or even Haley?"

"They didn't offer to help," Jill replied.

"And I suppose Carla did," Danielle said flatly.

"Yeah, she did," Jill stated.

Danielle sighed. "Jill, I think you're making a big mistake. Anyway, you told me you learned to ride in Colorado. So, why do you need lessons?"

Jill stood up and slung her bag over one shoulder. "I haven't ridden in months, so Carla's just giving me a couple of quick lessons. That's all. No big deal."

"So why haven't you told any of us, then?" Danielle asked.

"I don't know. I thought you guys—especially Tori— might get a little bent out of shape. You won't tell the others, will you? They won't understand."

"I'll keep it a secret if you want me to," Danielle said, "but don't say I didn't warn you."

"Let's find Nikki and give it to her now," Danielle said as she, Haley, Tori, and Jill left the arts and crafts shack the next morning.

Jill held the wrapped package out in front of her. "Do you think she'll be surprised?"

"Blown away is more like it," Tori replied with a grin. "She'll never in a million years guess what we've been doing."

"Yeah, but she's got to be suspicious," Haley added. "She asked me today at breakfast what I was making in arts and crafts and why I had stopped doing ceramics."

"What did you tell her?" Jill tucked the gift-wrapped package under her arm and glanced toward the lake, hoping for a glimpse of Ross. The boys' side of the camp was holding canoe races this morning.

"That I was painting a picture for Morgan," Haley replied, kicking off her shoes and wriggling her bare toes in the grass.

"When she asked me, I told her I was making earrings for Kathy Bart," Tori said with a giggle.

"The Sarge never wears earrings," Danielle pointed out. "She doesn't even have pierced ears."

"Exactly, but Nikki's been such a space cadet lately, I don't think she remembered that."

"Well, she's going to be so happy when she sees this!" Danielle said, patting the package.

"Nikki's over there," Tori said, pointing. "Look. Under that tree. Kit told her to work on lanyards outside today."

Nikki was sitting alone with a thoughtful expression on her face. A small pile of beads and colored plastic string lay in a box beside her.

"Surprise!" Jill cried, poking the package under Nikki's nose as the four girls ran up to her.

"For me?" Nikki looked from the package to Jill.

"From all of us," Jill added quickly.

Nikki shook her head in confusion, but began to smile. "But it's not my birthday or anything. . . ."

"We know *that*, silly!" Tori said.

"Open it!" Haley urged, jumping from foot to foot.

For one of the first times since she'd arrived in California, Jill felt the familiar warm feeling of being a real part of the Silver Blades crowd again.

As Nikki admired the wrapping paper, Jill smiled. It had been *her* idea to decorate a piece of brown paper with goofy magic marker drawings of pink flamingos—all on ice skates. "You guys even made the wrapping paper!" Nikki giggled.

Slowly, carefully, Nikki untied the bow, then neatly slid her finger under the tape on one end of the package.

"Don't take all day!" Haley urged.

Nikki's eyes were shining as she carefully unfolded the large piece of yellow felt. "What's this . . . ?" Her smile slowly vanished as she held up her present. The big wall hanging was decorated with felt giraffes, dinosaurs, elephants, and lots of other animals—all wearing skates and diapers.

"It's to celebrate your new brother or sister," Tori explained.

Jill watched in dismay as Nikki's face went pale.

"Don't you like it?" Danielle cried.

"We spent hours making it," Tori added.

"Yeah," Haley said, "and I cut out all the animal shapes and Tori glued them on. It was Jill's idea."

Nikki let out a muffled cry and stood up abruptly. "I'm sorry. I'm sorry," she repeated, trying to hold back the tears that were already forming. Jill couldn't believe the hurt in her eyes. Then, without saying another word, Nikki dropped the gift, along with the wrapping paper, onto the ground and ran off, sobbing, in the direction of their bunk.

"Whoops!" Haley made a face and looked around at the other girls. "We blew it."

"I don't get it," Tori said, shaking her head. "She could see we went to all that trouble. . . ." Tori sounded offended.

"What's wrong with her?" Danielle asked with concern.

Jill knelt on the grass and picked up the hanging, folding it neatly. She looked after Nikki and suddenly got it. "Nikki's been an only child for so long," Jill said slowly. "We're excited about the baby, but she's not. We haven't been listening to what she's been trying to tell us."

Haley stuffed the ribbon from the present into a

pocket of her overall-shorts. "You know," she began, "when Morgan was born, I think I hated her."

"I *still* think Nicholas hates me," Danielle joked lamely.

Jill scrambled to her feet. "Well, we're not helping Nikki standing around here. Come on. Let's go talk to her."

They found Nikki sprawled across her bed, her head buried in the pillow. Her body was shaking, and when the others arrived, she looked up. She was crying.

"Nikki, we're sorry." Jill sat down at the end of the bed and touched her friend gently on her shoulder.

Nikki looked at Jill miserably. "You don't understand. None of you do."

"We thought you'd love the present," Danielle said.

"I'm really sorry. It was really nice of you to make that wall hanging," Nikki apologized through her tears. "It's not the present. It's just . . . everything!"

"What do you mean?" Tori asked.

"All anyone thinks about anymore is that dumb baby. Even my parents. They've only written me once so far, and the postcard was all about how they can't wait for the new baby to come!" Nikki practically yelled. "Before I left home, all they talked about was the baby, the baby's room, the baby's clothes. . . . And now my best friends give me a present, and it's for the baby! I'm sick and tired of hearing about the baby. It's not even born yet and . . ." Her words trailed off.

"I've always had a big family, so, you're right, I

don't understand how you feel." Jill looked helplessly at Haley.

"But I do." Haley plopped down on the bunk next to Nikki and explained about Morgan and how awful it was at first to get used to having another kid get all the attention. Then Danielle shared stories her grandmother told her about how Nicholas had once broken all her toys because he was so upset when she'd gotten presents on her third birthday and he hadn't gotten any.

Nikki sniffed and sat a little straighter and listened. She bit her lip and looked up at Jill. "It's just that you guys were so excited about the baby. You never gave me a chance to talk. Everyone expected me to love the idea and I didn't . . . I don't. . . ."

"I'm sorry," Jill apologized. "I wish I'd listened to you better."

Nikki managed a weak smile. "I'm sorry I yelled at you guys, and . . ."

"It's okay," Jill assured her. "And we won't talk about the baby unless you want us to, okay?" She glanced at Danielle.

"Sure," Danielle agreed. "No more baby talk."

Nikki reached out and touched the wall hanging. Her smile widened enough to show her braces. "This *is* cute! Maybe I'll keep it for myself," she said, and laughed.

"That's the spirit," Haley cheered. "Fight for your rights. Make your parents feel guilty—it worked for me. When they bought Morgan a horse, I conned them into my first year of ice-skating lessons. Hey, this baby could mean lots of good things for you too, Nikki," Haley joked.

Nikki shook her head. Then she met Jill's glance, and the two of them grinned.

Once again, Jill realized, Haley had managed to make everyone laugh. But Jill was glad—it was good to feel close to Nikki again.

13

July 23

Dear Mom, Dad, and Company,

Time for the "I told you so's!" I will happily listen to every one of them. When I called you the first week we got here and told you how terrible it was to have Carla Benson in Bunk Nine, Mom said, "Jill, give Carla a chance." So I did. Am I ever glad! She's turned out to be a real friend. She's taught me how to ride—no, you don't need new glasses, Dad. I did say ride, as in H O R S E S!

I am going on a trail ride Sunday with a guy I met here—don't worry, other people will be along. He's a very experienced rider too. I won't get hurt. He's from Montana and wears a cowboy hat. We tried ice dancing together—I could really get into that. Gotta run. Time for swim class—or is it arts and crafts?

Love, Jill

"Hi," Jill said, as she put her lunch tray down onto her friends' table in the dining room the day before the color war.

Haley glanced up at her. "Here's our very own color-war captain!" She squeezed her chair closer to the wall to make room for Jill.

"We were just talking about you," Danielle said, and Jill froze midway through opening her milk carton. Had Dani told them about Carla?

"About you and the color war," Danielle added.

"Dani was confessing to a major case of butter-flies," Haley said. "She's as wired as if it were a *real* competition."

"Me too," Nikki joined in. Jill noticed Nikki looked more relaxed and cheerful. A letter was on Nikki's tray—she must have heard from her mother or Kyle, Jill thought.

"You'll be okay, Dani, once you get on the ice," Tori said confidently. "I can't wait for us to beat Carla and the yellow team. I've been practicing my double axel." Tori looked directly at Jill.

Jill took a deep breath. "Look, Tori, I really want the red team to win. And, as captain, I think you should do the double Lutz, not the double axel." Jill paused for a moment. "But it's not worth fighting about. So if you want to do the double axel for the skate-off, do it."

The others stared at Jill.

"Really?" Tori asked, sounding shocked.

Jill shrugged. "Really. It seems to mean a lot to you to do this jump in the skate-off, so go ahead. Our friendship is more important than the color war."

"Thanks," Tori said. "You'll be surprised. I'm going to land it."

"I hope so," Danielle said under her breath.

"Patrick told me that the boys' competition happens after ours," Haley said. "It'll be fun to watch them skate."

Jill listened as the others talked about the boys' color-war teams. Soon the conversation switched to the trail ride scheduled for after lunch. All the campers had had the opportunity to choose from a list of special activities for this period. Danielle, Nikki, Tori, and Haley all had signed up for the trail ride. As the girls talked about how beautiful the trails were, Jill wished she could tell them about the progress she was making on horseback.

"What did you sign up for, Jill?" Nikki asked.

"Arts and crafts," Jill replied. Suddenly she had a great idea. "I just remembered something," she said as she stood up quickly. "I'll catch up with you guys later." She picked up her tray and dumped the remains of her lunch into a nearby trash can.

She quickly made her way toward Carla's table. As she walked past it, she said quietly, "Meet me outside."

Carla nodded slowly. "Okay. What's wrong?"

"Nothing. Just follow me out."

Jill slipped out the side entrance of the dining hall, hoping that none of her friends would come out and see her talking to Carla. A minute or two later Carla joined her.

"Okay. What's the mystery?" Carla asked, looking eager.

"I just had a great idea," Jill said excitedly. "There's a trail ride scheduled for this afternoon. Want to go?"

"I'm already signed up for that trail ride," Carla answered. "Don't tell me you want to go."

Jill nodded. "Haley and the others are going riding this afternoon, and I want to go too. I also want to tell them the truth. I'm sick of lying about everything."

"Oh, I see. . . ." Carla raised her eyebrows. "But why not just tell them? Why would you want to ride with them?"

"They're my friends!" Jill replied. "Besides, it would be fun to surprise them. Listen, how about I meet you at the stables in twenty minutes?"

"Okay. I've got to find Sharon and Sandy anyway. They're probably wondering why I just ran out of the dining room."

"Carla, there's something else I need to ask you," Jill said suddenly.

"Sure. What?" Carla asked.

"You promised me that you wouldn't tell anyone about our riding lessons," Jill said. "So how did Sharon and Sandy find out?"

"I didn't break my promise," Carla insisted. "They, uh, just sort of found out."

"But how?" Jill asked.

"They wanted to know where I was one afternoon. And when they asked Merry, she told them that I was giving you riding lessons," Carla explained.

"Okay," Jill said, nodding. Carla's story sounded as if it could be true, and Carla had certainly proved herself to be a good friend this whole week.

While Carla headed back into the dining hall, Jill ran all the way to her bunk. Good. No one was there. She changed into boots and jeans. Then she hurried over to the arts and crafts shack to get permission from Kit to go riding instead. Last week the tennis counselor had lectured her about sticking to the schedule. The last thing she needed was to get in trouble for riding today.

A few minutes later, as Jill jogged to the stable, the same thought kept repeating in her mind: I'm going on my first trail ride!

"Hey, watch it!" Ross cried as Jill rounded the corner of the barn and practically ran into him. Ross shoved his cowboy hat back on his head and burst out laughing. "We have to stop bumping into each other this way!"

Jill smiled while her mind raced into high gear. "What are you doing here?" she asked.

"Trail ride," he replied.

"Me too," Jill said. Uh-oh, she was thinking. I hope he doesn't see me making any big mistakes.

"The trail ride leaves at one," Ross said. "Practically everyone is ready." He gestured with his head toward the ring. Patrick McGuire, Alex Beekman, and a boy named Jerry Dias were already on horseback. Two girls from Bunk Seven were petting their horses, tightening girths, and talking. But Jill's friends still hadn't arrived.

Just then Merry and Carla came out of the barn. "Oh, hi," Carla called out. She smiled at Ross, then took Jill's arm and steered her away. "He doesn't know you've been taking lessons, does he?" she whispered.

Jill glanced back toward Ross. "No . . ."

"Come on," Carla said. "I've already saddled my horse. Let's get Smokey ready." She set off toward the barn. Jill followed, leaving Ross talking with Merry.

Jill began to groom Smokey. She hadn't gotten very far when Ross entered the next stall. The large pinto pony in the next stall was already saddled. He snorted happily at the sight of Ross.

"This will be great," Ross said, leaning over the top of the stall and grinning at Jill. "Are we still on for Sunday?"

"Wouldn't miss it," Jill replied, hoping that by then she'd feel more confident. She watched Ross amble out of the stable, leading his horse by the reins.

Ten minutes later Jill led Smokey out of the barn. She had saddled and bridled him without any help.

She felt really proud of herself. Smokey had quietly opened his mouth when she'd held the bit in front of him, and he hadn't minded when she'd tightened the girth. Quickly she tested the leather strap that held the saddle on. It still felt nice and snug. No need to worry.

Just as Jill led Smokey out of the barn, she saw Tori and the others walking toward her across the field. Jill couldn't wait to see the expressions on her friends' faces when they saw her standing by her horse.

Tori stopped by the paddock gate and stared at her, and Haley's brown eyes widened with surprise.

Nikki looked astonished. "Jill," she said, "I thought you hated horses. Are you coming with us?"

"You bet," Jill said with a smile. "We can all go trail riding together."

"Great!" Nikki said. She and the other girls hurried toward the barn, but Danielle hung back.

"Come on, Dani," Tori yelled over her shoulder. "Hurry up."

"In a minute," Danielle replied, but she didn't move. She just stared at Jill. "Are you sure you're good enough to go trail riding?" she asked. "Isn't it too soon? I mean, you've only just started riding. . . ."

Jill knew Danielle was concerned about her. "I hope I'm good enough," she replied honestly. "I'm ready to try the trail anyway."

"I'll ride next to you," Danielle offered. "In case you need help."

When Danielle ran off to the barn, Jill went into the

riding ring. Carla was already there. She was mounted on a white filly named Blizzard and was trotting
around the ring. Ross, Patrick, Alex, Jerry, and the two
girls from Bunk Seven headed out through the corral
toward the woods. "Wait for everyone at the edge of
the woods," Merry called after them.

"You look more comfortable," Carla said to Jill,
reaching out and patting Smokey's head.

"Not so loud!" Jill warned. "I want to surprise my
friends. Maybe you could go on ahead, and I'll catch
up."

"Right!" Carla said, her mouth forming into a narrow line. "You want me to drop out of the picture
now that your Silver Blades friends are around. Is
that it?"

Jill was speechless. She was about to say something
about how much she appreciated Carla's help, but
just then Tori walked up, leading a chestnut gelding.
"Uh . . ." Jill could feel the panic rising.

"What are you doing here, Carla?" Tori asked.

"Taking the trail ride," Carla said curtly. "I'm going
to catch up with the others now. See you *all* soon."
She caught Jill's eye, then kicked her horse's flanks
and cantered out into the open field.

Tori headed back into the stable, and with a sigh
Jill watched Carla ride off. Jill didn't want Carla to
think she had dumped her. She still wanted to be
friends. She'd have to find a way to explain later.
Meanwhile Jill needed to get up on Smokey. After
several tries she finally hoisted herself up. She had

just settled into the saddle and taken the reins in her hands when the others emerged from the barn, leading their horses.

Tori and the others mounted quickly and rode up to Jill. Tori looked upset. "I just talked to Dani. I can't believe you took riding lessons from Carla!"

Jill groaned. Her secret was almost completely out in the open now. "Carla's been giving me some pointers," she said casually. "Since I've only been on horseback a few times in Denver."

Do you really feel okay about coming trail riding with us, Jill?" Haley said. "You don't have to, you know."

"I'll do fine," Jill insisted, wishing her friends would stop worrying so much. "Carla knows what she's doing. Wait till you see her ride. She's up ahead with the rest of the group."

Merry rode up on her champagne-colored mare and smiled encouragingly at Jill. "I guess you guys are the last of the bunch. Let's line up and start out slowly. The others are waiting up ahead."

Merry went to the head of the line, and Jill gathered up her reins, anxious to get going.

"Hey, you guys, go easy on Jill, okay?" Merry turned in her saddle and yelled behind her. "She's still a beginner, and I don't want her breaking anything."

"I'll ride behind her," Danielle promised.

"Okay. Let's go!" Haley yelled.

As they filed out across the field Tori glanced back

at Jill again and shook her head slowly. Jill urged Smokey forward and ignored her friend. Everything has worked out almost perfectly, Jill thought. I don't have to lie anymore, and I'm on a trail ride with all my friends and the cutest guy in the camp.

Once the group was together on the trail, Jill began to relax. So far they were only walking because the trail was rocky and narrow. She sighed with relief. This was going to be really easy. Why had she worried so much? As they rode, she kept an eye on the front of the group, where Ross was. Somehow Carla had managed to plant herself next to him. Jill wondered what they were talking about.

"You're doing great, Jill!" Tori rode up behind her. "I'm sorry for what I said back in the ring."

"That's okay," Jill said. She smiled at Tori.

Five minutes later Carla and Ross broke into a fast trot, and the other riders followed suit.

Jill gave the instruction to Smokey, doing her best to keep from bouncing in the saddle. It wasn't that easy, after all, especially out on the bumpy trail. And Smokey was going much faster than he had in the riding ring.

Just as Jill was beginning to panic, the trail got narrow again. Everyone slowed to a walk, and Jill caught her breath. But it was only a short break.

"There are some trees lying across the path," Carla called back to the group. "They're great fun to jump."

"There's probably a way around the logs," Danielle whispered to Jill as she maneuvered her chestnut mare beside Smokey.

"Good," Jill murmured.

"Only experienced riders may jump!" Merry called out in warning.

"Let's go!" Carla dug her heels into her horse's sides and cantered off. Ross did the same.

"Jill, don't follow them!" Danielle said.

"Don't worry," Jill replied. "We'll go around the logs, like you said."

Luckily Danielle was right. They were able to swing off the trail and avoid going over the logs. Haley and Tori jumped them, and Nikki followed Jill and Danielle.

Now Jill could barely see Carla and Ross, who were way up ahead on the trail. She felt a stab of jealousy. It wasn't fair. Carla was getting Ross all to herself because she could ride as well as he did.

They caught up with the others when the trail opened up into a large meadow.

"You okay, Jill?" Ross called out.

"Of course she is," Carla replied. "Come on, let's get going."

Ross shot Jill an anxious look. "Hey, not so fast. There's no hurry." He gathered up his reins and glanced at Carla. "You go on ahead. I'll ride with Jill."

"Oh, come on," Carla said quickly. "This is a great field. Why don't we let the horses run? Jill will only hold you back. You do know, Ross, that she's never ridden a horse before this week, don't you?"

"What are you talking about?" Ross said. "Jill can ride."

"Only since five days ago," Carla answered loudly. "I've been giving her lessons all week."

Jill was too stunned to answer. She couldn't believe that Carla had just betrayed her—and in front of Ross! Carla had *promised* not to say anything!

"Jill?" Tori said, her voice filled with concern. "What's going on?"

Jill took a deep breath. There was nothing to do now but tell the whole truth. "Carla's right," Jill admitted, holding back her tears. "I lied about riding in Denver. I felt so out of it, being the only one who couldn't ride. I just made up that story so you guys wouldn't give me a hard time." Jill stared at the ground. She was too embarrassed even to look at Ross.

Her friends were silent for a moment, then Tori spoke up. "It's all right, Jill. But you shouldn't be on this trail ride now. It could really be dangerous for you."

"Tori's right," Danielle said. "Why don't you head back to the stable with me now, and Haley and Tori can ride ahead and tell Merry. Okay?"

Jill took a deep breath. "That's probably a good idea," she agreed. At that moment she wanted to get as far away from Carla and Ross as possible.

As Haley and Tori headed across the meadow toward Merry, Carla announced, "Well, I'm not going to have my trail ride ruined just because Jill can't ride. I'm cantering!" And with that, Carla dug her heels into her horse's sides and took off across the meadow.

Suddenly Smokey, who was standing next to Carla's horse, pricked up his ears. And before anyone, especially Jill, realized what was happening, Smokey took off like a rocket after Carla's horse!

"Help!" Jill cried out. She frantically pulled back on Smokey's reins. But something was wrong. Smokey wouldn't stop. Jill heard Danielle's worried shout behind her, but it was too late. Smokey began to canter. This was the first time Jill had ever cantered, and it was frightening. Cantering was much faster than trotting, and Smokey was increasing his speed with every stride. Jill's mind went numb. She had to concentrate on staying in the saddle. The wind whipped Smokey's mane across her face, stinging her eyes, but she didn't let go. She didn't dare.

"Jill, Jill! Watch out!" Haley yelled. Dimly Jill heard the warning voice behind her.

Haley yelled again. "Get your feet out of your stirrups!"

But Smokey's speed only increased. And as the horse raced after Carla, Jill held on to the reins for dear life.

15

"**G**et your feet out of your stirrups—*now!*" Haley yelled as she galloped up to Jill.

This time Jill understood what Haley was saying. But why? What was wrong with her stirrups? She hesitated, not sure what to do. If she took her feet out of the stirrups, she'd fall off for sure. But why did Haley want her to fall off? It made no sense.

"Jill! Your feet! Get them out! Now!" Haley sounded almost hysterical.

The fear in Haley's voice finally jarred Jill into action. She pulled her legs back and kicked both stirrups free. A split second later Smokey's head went down and he bucked, throwing his body into the air. Jill flew out of the saddle and landed on the ground with a hard thump.

Jill gasped and tried to sit up. The breath had been

knocked out of her. Dimly she heard horses' hooves racing toward her, and then she was aware of voices asking if she was hurt. She was too breathless to speak.

"Jill!" Danielle sounded really scared. "Are you okay?"

"Haley, go and catch Smokey." Tori jumped off her horse and took charge. She crouched down beside Jill and said, "Don't move. Wait till you get your breath back. Someone get Merry!" Tori shouted over her shoulder.

"Are you all right?" Nikki sounded close to tears.

Jill finally found her voice. "It's okay," she croaked. "I'm all right, really." Then she slowly stretched out her legs and sat up. Nothing felt broken, but she was definitely bruised, and her left elbow was throbbing.

"Stay right there!" Merry commanded a few minutes later as she approached on horseback with Ross and the others. The counselor quickly dismounted and handed the reins to Tori. She bent down next to Jill. "Are you sure you're okay?" She did a quick check of Jill's arms and legs. "You didn't hit your head?"

"No," Jill replied. "I think I'm fine—just a little shaky."

Merry examined Jill's right arm, where the sleeve was torn at the elbow. "It's just a bad cut," Merry said, then guided Jill over to a log and sat her down. The other kids stood watching, perfectly silent. "Now, exactly what happened here?" Merry asked.

"I was about to go back to the stable with Dani,

and my horse just took off after Carla's horse. Smokey wouldn't pay attention when I tried to stop him," Jill said in a very low voice. She watched as Haley rode back into the field, leading Smokey. "And Haley kept yelling at me to take my feet out of the stirrups. What was wrong with my stirrups?" she asked as the other girl approached.

"Nothing," Haley said. "It was your saddle."

"The saddle?" Jill was puzzled. "I don't get it."

"Look at Smokey's saddle," Haley explained. "See how far forward it is. It's almost up to his ears!"

Jill looked. Haley was right. The saddle was nearly onto Smokey's neck. "Is that what made him throw me off?"

"Yup. You were probably driving him nuts. Horses hate it when a rider is out of balance." Haley turned back toward the horse. She took hold of the leather girth and pulled on it. "See this? It's way too loose."

"But I tightened it as much as I could," Jill protested. She remembered checking the girth before they left the barn. It had been plenty tight enough then.

Haley said, "You should always check your girth again, after you get on."

"Why?" Carla hadn't told Jill about that.

"Because horses hate having their girth tightened, and most of them will blow their stomachs out while you're doing it," Haley explained. "If you don't know what they're doing, you end up with a very loose girth once you get in the saddle."

"Oh, I get it," Jill said. Poor Smokey. No wonder he had thrown her.

"If you hadn't taken your feet out of the stirrups, you'd probably have been dragged halfway across the field," Merry said quietly. "Your foot would most likely have gotten stuck in the stirrup when Smokey bucked. You were lucky Haley saw what was happening."

Jill shuddered, thinking what might have happened if Haley hadn't been watching out for her. She'd have probably broken her arm, or even worse, her legs! Her skating career could have been finished.

"Haley, thanks," Jill finally said. "I owe you one." She slowly reached toward Haley and squeezed her arm. "I really mean it. I don't know what I'd have done if I'd broken something."

Haley shrugged, and flashed Jill a smile. "It was nothing. You'd have done the same for me."

Merry folded her arms across her chest. She looked from Carla, to Haley, to Jill. Jill squirmed under her glance. "This is pretty serious stuff, guys," the counselor said. "Carla, you misled me about Jill's riding experience. I was under the impression she'd had more lessons before you took her into the ring. And you should have told Jill about the girth—"

"I didn't forget on purpose!" Carla interrupted, looking defensive.

"I know you didn't, and I'm sure you won't make that mistake again. But I'm going to ground you—"

"That's not fair," Carla charged, and glared at Jill. "It's her fault too."

Merry silenced Carla with a look, then turned to Jill. "You too, Jill. Lying about your riding experience was a stupid—and dangerous—thing to do. You could have been really hurt today. So tonight you and Carla are both grounded."

"It's movie night!" Carla wailed.

"Right," Merry said.

Jill was silent.

"Nikki and Tori," the counselor went on, "why don't you walk Jill back to the stables to clean up. Walk your horses back too. Ross, you catch up with the rest of the riders and go on ahead. I'll be right with you. Carla and Haley, take Smokey and your horses back to the barn. Be sure to cool Smokey down."

After everyone had left, Jill, Nikki, and Tori slowly walked back to the stables. Every inch of Jill ached, but she was so grateful she wasn't hurt that she almost didn't care. Jill thanked her friends again. "I don't know what I'd do without you guys," she admitted.

"Probably break every bone in your body!" Tori remarked with a laugh. "Fortunately you've always been a pretty hard-headed person." She tapped Jill lightly on the head, and Jill leaned into Tori for a moment, happy to have such good friends.

Later that night Jill sat cross-legged on her bed and attempted to write a letter to Bronya. She avoided looking across the bunk at Sharon's bed, where Carla sat, flipping through a magazine. Tapping her pen against her box of stationery, Jill tried to think of what to write after "Dear Bronya," but she couldn't concentrate.

After a few minutes the tension in the bunk was too much for Jill to bear. "I just don't get it, Carla. Why did you embarrass me like that today?"

Carla didn't glance up. "Don't blame me. This mess is your fault. You should have known better. You shouldn't have gone trail riding with us. You just aren't good enough."

"Not good enough!" Jill cried, her dark eyes flashing with anger. "You're the one who said I was riding well. How come you changed your mind?"

"I said *that*?" Carla asked, her voice dripping with sarcasm. "I don't remember."

"I thought you were my friend, but I guess I was wrong," Jill said softly.

"And I thought you were cool," Carla replied angrily. "I really thought you'd changed, but you haven't."

"What's that supposed to mean?" Jill challenged.

Carla took a deep breath and looked directly at Jill. "At first I was really jealous that you were chosen right off to go to the Ice Academy. I'm stuck on a waiting list. It's possible I won't get into the Academy this year. Then I thought if we became friends, you could talk the directors into getting me off the waiting list."

Jill stared at her. "You mean, you were just using me?"

"You didn't let me finish," Carla said quickly. She

hesitated for a moment. "I admit it, I was going to use you to get into the Academy. And that was mean. But when I got to know you and we started spending time at the stables together, I really liked you. I really wanted to be your friend."

"So what happened?" Jill asked. "A real friend wouldn't break a promise and tell something she swore she wouldn't tell. A real friend wouldn't put me in danger."

"I didn't mean to put you in danger—really," Carla said. "But I couldn't . . . I can't believe you asked me to leave so you could hang out with your old friends. You really hurt my feelings."

Jill sighed, and hopped down off her top bunk. She walked over to Carla and sat next to her on the bed. "Carla, look. I didn't mean to hurt your feelings at the stable. But I really didn't want my friends to know I couldn't ride. It was stupid of me. I'm sorry."

Carla was silent for a few minutes. "Okay," she mumbled finally.

At that moment the bunk door banged open. Nikki, Danielle, Tori, and Haley hurried inside.

"What are you guys doing back from the movie so early?" Jill asked, surprised to see them.

"We couldn't have fun at the movies knowing you were sitting in this stuffy old bunk," Danielle said.

"So we decided that if you were grounded, then we'd all be grounded too," Nikki added.

"Or at least keep you company," Tori said with a smile.

"I'm going to hang out on the porch," Carla announced.

Jill watched her go, wondering if she should invite the other girl to stay.

Tori made a face behind Carla's back. "Aren't you furious at her, Jill?"

"No," Jill answered truthfully. "I actually still like her. I'm just not sure the two of us were meant to be friends." She grinned. "Not like all of us."

She gave each one of them a big hug. Not one of them had to be here with her, but they'd stayed by her side like true friends—even though she had lied to them. Their friendship was really special, and Jill wondered how she could have doubted that all week.

After she hugged Tori, her friend hugged her back. "I'm sorry."

Jill stared at her. "What for?"

"For being jealous and being a big pain about the color war. I hate it that you're going to the Ice Academy and I'm not," Tori continued. "I've tried to stop feeling that way, but I can't help it. And when you were chosen color-war captain instead of me, I guess I sort of lost it."

"That's okay," Jill said. "I know you're jealous and I know that your mom puts a lot of pressure on you."

Tori grinned. "Thanks. Don't worry about color war—I've been practicing that double axel nonstop."

"Oh, Jill," Danielle broke in. "It's so great having you with us again. I wish you didn't live in Denver."

"It won't be forever," Jill promised. Then she glanced

at Haley and decided that while everyone was apologizing, she might as well add one more.

"Haley, I'm really sorry it's taken me so long to treat you like a real friend."

Haley blushed and looked away. "That's all right," she said in a muffled voice.

"No, it's not," Jill insisted. "It took me a while to give you a chance. I was jealous that you were hanging out with all my old friends. It seemed like you'd taken my place."

Haley's eyes widened. "Are you kidding? All those three do is talk about you and how well you skate and how funny you are and how much they wish you'd move back to Seneca Hills. They're always saying they miss the days when it was you four."

"Well, now it's us *five*," Jill said firmly. She wrapped an arm around the other skater. "Welcome to the best part of Silver Blades."

At that, cheers filled the bunk and drifted on out into the cool California night.

16

Dear Jill—
Hope you are feeling better. I know you will be
the star tonight. I can't wait to cheer you on from
the stands. I hope the red team and its terrific—and
brave—captain win the girls' color war.
                    Ross Barrett

"Go, red team, go!" Jill and her friends cried the next
evening in the Redwood Skating Camp arena. The
skating rink was packed with campers, all of them
rooting for either the yellow team or the red team.

Jill held her breath as Haley leaped into the air,
touched the toes of each of her skates with her fingers

in a split position, and landed back on the ice to thunderous applause.

Then Sharon Groves performed her split jump for the yellow team. She received the same high score as Haley did.

"Both teams are tied now," Haley said to her friends as she watched Sharon skate off the ice.

"We've only got two more skaters to go," Jill declared. "I can't believe how close this competition has been all night." Jill had won points for the red team earlier with a perfect double-Lutz jump.

"Let's go, red team!" Nikki cheered.

Robin Turner announced the next move, "A flying camel sitspin. Danielle Panati will perform it for the red team, and Erin Clancy for the yellow team."

The audience yelled and cheered, and Jill crossed her fingers. Because it was such a tricky jump, it was often called the death drop.

Danielle skated toward the center of the ice. With a strong upward movement she lifted her right leg forward and leaped into the air, her legs spread apart in a split. Then she landed on her right skate and dropped down into a sitspin position. She twirled around in a blur, and her arms raised above her head.

Jill and the rest of the red team clapped and cheered. A moment later Danielle's score was announced. She had received eight points out of a possible ten. Happily Danielle skated back to the edge of the ice and joined the rest of her team.

"Really great!" Nikki said with a wide grin. Nikki had performed her layback spin earlier.

Tori handed Danielle a cup of ice water, and they all turned their attention back toward the ice. Erin was ready to try the death drop.

"Nope." Haley shook her head when Erin had completed the movement. "She didn't get high enough."

"I don't know," Jill murmured. "It looked pretty good to me."

The judges apparently agreed with Haley and deducted two points from Erin's score.

"The red team is ahead by two!" Danielle shouted, jumping up and down with excitement.

"Our last event in the skate-off," Robin announced, "will be the double axel. Tori Carsen will perform the jump for the red team and Carla Benson, for the yellow team."

"Hurrah, Tori!" Haley cheered.

Tori stepped onto the ice and circled the rink several times. From where she was standing, Jill could see how hard Tori was concentrating. Come on, Tori, you can do it, Jill cheered silently.

Jill held her breath as Tori sprang into the difficult jump on the outside edge of her left skate. She began the required two-and-a-half rotations, just barely making it all the way around twice before she started to come down. But Tori managed to cheat the final half rotation and land on a wobbly right outside edge.

"Amazing!" Jill shouted, giving Tori a big hug when she skated off the ice. The jump wasn't perfect—but Tori had landed it for the first time! "I'm so proud of you!" Jill told her friend.

"I told you I could do a double axel," Tori replied. "I'm just glad I was right," she added with a laugh.

Carla readied herself for her turn at the double axel. Her yellow skating dress sparkled in the rink's lights as she leaped high in the air, rotated tightly, and landed smoothly seconds later.

Carla's form was brilliant, and Jill clapped hard along with the rest of the campers. Whatever she thought of Carla as a person—and the jury was still out on that one—Jill really appreciated great skating. And Carla was skating her personal best tonight.

"Look, here're the scores!" Nikki cried. Jill held her breath and turned to look. Had the red team been able to maintain their lead and win the color war?

"Oh, no," Tori muttered. Carla had received two more points than Tori.

"That means it's a tie," Danielle said.

At that moment Robin Turner reached for her microphone and announced, "We have a tie, so we are going to have a tiebreaker. Our captains, Jill and Carla, will each perform the same jump, which I will choose with the judges. The winner of this event will also decide the winner of the color war."

"You're going to win, Jill! I know it," Tori said.

"Only if the last jump isn't a triple," Jill muttered to herself.

Danielle heard her. "What's wrong?"

"We've already done about every jump on our level," Jill said. "The few that are left are definitely not my strong points!" She saw the judges nod in her direction. "I'm up," she murmured. "Here goes. Wish me luck!"

With cries of encouragement ringing in her ears, Jill tugged down the sleeve of her sleek red unitard and took to the ice.

"Go, Jill! Go, Jill, go!" Haley, Nikki, and Tori chanted from the side of the rink. Jill circled the ice, concentrating on her warm-up and blocking out the sound of the crowd. She was still bruised and stiff from her fall, though the evening of competitive skating had actually made her muscles feel better.

When Jill felt limber, she skated with Carla across to the judges to find out what the jump was going to be. She wondered if Ross was somewhere in the audience. He had left her a note in her skate bag saying he'd be cheering for her, but she hadn't spotted him in the crowd. She wondered if their date for tomorrow was still on. She still hadn't faced him since her disastrous trail ride.

I've got to stop thinking about Ross, she told herself sternly. Right now I've got to concentrate.

"The last jump will be a triple salchow, and Jill will skate first," Robin announced. "Good luck!"

There were several different preparations for this jump, and Jill decided on clockwise back crossovers. When she felt ready to try the jump, she stepped onto her takeoff leg and forced herself to think of nothing but the triple salchow.

It was over in seconds. Jill landed firmly and cleanly to the sound of wild cheering and clapping. She'd done it! She'd completed an almost perfect triple salchow. "All right!" she shouted, and pumped her arms in the air.

"Fantastic!" Danielle cheered as Jill skated up to her teammates. "I knew you could do it!"

A hush descended over the arena as Carla skated around the rink, finishing her warm-up. Her yellow skirt fluttered against her long legs as she prepared for her triple salchow.

Jill held her breath as she watched Carla take off. It looked at first as if Carla hadn't jumped high enough, but she increased the pace of her rotations and landed solidly on the ice.

"It's going to be a really close call," Haley said as the audience clapped for Carla.

"Oh, hurry up, hurry up!" Tori shouted in the direction of the judging stand.

Jill shivered with excitement.

Finally Arleen Watson, the camp director and head judge, announced, "We have a first in the history of Redwood Skating Camp. This year color war is a tie. Congratulations to both the red and yellow teams!"

"A tie!" Tori cried.

"Hey, that's cool," Haley said.

Both teams were called onto the ice to receive their prizes—big red and yellow ribbons. As Arleen handed Jill and Carla their ribbons, Carla turned to Jill and said, "Congratulations. You skated great today."

Jill smiled at Carla. "Thanks. You skated great too. We both won."

⌒ ⌒

"I can't believe camp is already half over!" Jill exclaimed as she walked arm in arm with her friends toward the campfire later that evening.

The campfire was roaring by the time they got there. The smell of roasting hot dogs and marshmallows mingled with the piney smell of the clear California night air.

A group from Bunk Six made room for them on the lakeside of the fire. Jill settled down with her friends and looked around.

"Guess who's here?" Danielle whispered in Jill's ear a moment later. She pointed across the bonfire.

Jill looked through the flames. Sure enough, it was Ross, sitting with a bunch of guys. He was scanning the crowd of campers.

"I bet he's looking for you," Nikki told Jill, then popped a couple of marshmallows on a stick and crouched closer to the fire to toast them.

"Dream on," Jill replied, but her heart started beating faster. Ross had just spotted her. He got up and headed in their direction.

"He's coming over," Danielle whispered.

"Can I sit down?" Ross asked Jill, rocking back and forth in his cowboy boots and looking a little shy.

"Yeah . . . sure," Jill stammered. She moved closer

to Danielle, and Ross sat down between Jill and Nikki.

"That was really great skating," he said. The admiration in his voice was unmistakable. Jill suddenly felt very proud. She was glad he'd seen her do her best.

"Thanks," Jill said, and was immediately tongue-tied.

"So how about our date?" he asked.

"What?" Jill said.

"It's still on, right?"

"No, I mean . . . yes." Jill groped for the right words.

"Is this *no* you can't come, or *yes* you will?" Ross teased.

Jill hesitated. There was no way she was going to get back on a horse again—even for Ross.

He seemed to read her mind. "Look, why don't we try something else. We don't have to go riding. How about rollerblading?" Ross asked.

"You're on!" Jill's grin widened. "That's something I *really* am great at."

Then, before she had time to take another breath, Ross leaned toward her and kissed her quickly on the cheek. He jumped up and disappeared into the crowd.

Tori, Haley, Danielle, and Nikki practically pounced on her. "He *kissed* you!" Nikki cried. Danielle pretended to swoon. "Gross," Haley teased her.

But Jill didn't mind. It was her first kiss, and she'd never forget it.

17

Dear Bronya,

Camp is now half over—two more weeks and I'll be back at the Ice Academy. And, boy, do I have a story to tell you when I get there! I'll give you a hint, though—it involves me on a horse and then me flying off a horse!

My date with Ross is still on for tomorrow, but we're definitely NOT going riding. Whew! Except after the little prank Haley and I played tonight on Ross, Alex, and Patrick's bunk, I have my fingers crossed that Ross will still be speaking to me! Get this—at the campfire tonight the boys in Bunk Twelve took their sneakers off and left them near the fire. Tori, Nikki, and Dani distracted the boys

*while Haley and I stuck marshmallows in the toes.
You should have seen their faces when they put
them back on! It was totally great. Haley and I are
quite a team, which should make it an interesting
two weeks!*

Keep the letters coming!
Your friend,
Jill

Don't miss any of the previous books in the Silver Blades series:

#1: Breaking the Ice

Nikki Simon is thrilled when she makes the Silver Blades skating club. But Nikki quickly realizes that being a member of Silver Blades is going to be tougher than she thought. Both Nikki and another skater, Tori Carsen, have to land the double flip jump. But how far will Tori go to make sure that *she* lands it first?

#2: In the Spotlight

Danielle Panati has always worked hard at her skating, and it's definitely starting to pay off. Danielle's just won the lead role in the Silver Blades Fall Ice Spectacular. Rehearsals go well at first, then the other members of Silver Blades start noticing that Danielle is acting strange. Is it the pressure of being in the spotlight— or does Danielle have a secret that she doesn't want to share?

#3: The Competition

Tori Carsen loves skating when her mother isn't around, but as soon as her mother appears at the rink, skating becomes a nightmare. Mrs. Carsen argues with Tori's coaches and embarrasses her in front of the rest of the club. When Tori and several other members of Silver Blades go to Lake Placid for a regional competition, her mother becomes even more demanding. Could it have anything to do with a mysterious stranger who keeps showing up at the rink?

4: Going for the Gold

It's a dream come true! Jill's going to the famous figure skating center in Colorado. But the training is *much* tougher than Jill ever expected, and Kevin, a really cute skater at the school, has a plan that's sure to get her into *big* trouble. Could this be the end of Jill's skating career?

5: The Perfect Pair

Nikki Simon and Alex Beekman are the perfect pair on the ice. But off the ice there's a big problem. Suddenly Alex is sending Nikki gifts and asking her out on dates. Nikki wants to be Alex's partner in pairs but not his girlfriend. Will she lose Alex when she tells him? Can Nikki's friends in Silver Blades find a way to save her friendship with Alex *and* her skating career?

6: Skating Camp

Summer's here, and Jill Wong can't wait to join her best friends from Silver Blades at skating camp. It's going to be just like old times. But things have changed since Jill left Silver Blades to train at a famous ice academy. Tori and Danielle are spending all their time with another skater, Haley Arthur, and Nikki has a big secret that she won't share with anyone. Has Jill lost her best friends forever?

7: The Ice Princess

Tori's favorite skating superstar, Elyse Taylor, is in town, and she's staying with Tori! When Elyse promises to teach Tori her famous spin, Tori's sure they'll become the best of friends. But Elyse isn't the sweet champion everyone thinks she is. And she's out to make real problems for Tori!

8: Rumors at the Rink

Haley can't believe it—Kathy Bart, her favorite coach in the whole world, is quitting Silver Blades! Haley's sure it's all her fault. Why didn't she listen when everyone told her to stop playing practical jokes on Kathy? With Kathy gone, Haley knows she'll never win the next big competition. She has to make Kathy change her mind—no matter what. But will Haley's secret plan work?

Ice Has Never Been So Hot—
with
Silver Blades!

Read the exciting behind-the-scenes stories of four talented young skaters entering the world of competitive figure skating.

Order any or all of these hot new stories you won't want to keep on ice for long. Just check off the titles you want, then fill out and mail the order form below.

☐	0-553-48134-7	**BREAKING THE ICE**	$3.50/$4.50 Can.
☐	0-553-48135-5	**IN THE SPOTLIGHT**	$3.50/$4.50 Can.
☐	0-553-48136-3	**THE COMPETITION**	$3.50/$4.50 Can.
☐	0-553-48137-1	**GOING FOR THE GOLD**	$3.50/$4.50 Can.
☐	0-553-48194-0	**THE PERFECT PAIR**	$3.50/$4.50 Can.
☐	0-553-48198-3	**SKATING CAMP**	$3.50/$4.50 Can.
☐	0-553-48289-0	**THE ICE PRINCESS**	$3.50/$4.50 Can.
☐	0-553-48293-9	**RUMORS AT THE RINK**	$3.50/$4.50 Can.

Bantam Doubleday Dell
Books For Young Readers

BDD BOOKS FOR YOUNG READERS
2451 South Wolf Road
Des Plaines, IL 60018

Please send me the items I have checked above. I am enclosing $_____
(please add $2.50 to cover postage and handling).
Send check or money order, no cash or C.O.D.s please.

NAME _____

ADDRESS _____

CITY _____ STATE _____ ZIP _____

Please allow four to six weeks for delivery.
Prices and availability subject to change without notice.   BFYR 114 2/95